HUCKLEBERRY DICK

A LOVE STORY
DETECTIVE MYSTERY

ROD MARTIN

I0781066

Copyright © 2023 by Rod Martin

All rights reserved. No parts of this book may be used or reproduced by any means, graphic, electronic, and mechanical, including photocopying, recording, taping, or by any information storage retrieval system, without the written permission of the publisher except in the case of brief quotations embodied in critical articles and reviews.

ISBN: 978-1-963565-57-7 (Paperback)

ISBN: 978-1-963565-58-4 (E-book)

Library of Congress Control Number: 2024926684

Printed in the United States of America

Published by:

info@thequippyquill.com
(302) 295-2278

Dedication:

For Darrel Martin.
Darrel would do it.
R.I.P.

Warning: This fictional work contains sex, drugs, violence and adult
situations (so it should be fun).

CHAPTERS

Preface

No, this is not going to be a mix of Huckleberry Finn and Moby Dick. No great pipe smokin' river-raftin' whales will be hurt in the making of this novel. If Moby Dick was about searching for something, this is too, sort of. If Huckleberry Finn is about true friendship and breaking racial barriers, well that's asking a lot from what passes for literature in this day and age so cut me some slack.

I type these words and a microprocessor tells the monitor what pixels to activate producing letters in lines unless I'm distracted by Hawaiian sunrise, towering mountains, or the birdsong of my paradise home but I digress. I wander.

You'll be lucky if you get sentence structure and punctuation, let alone a plot or any meaningful connection to reality as you sees it and certainly my perspective is an implied bias.

I am finding my own voice. And just as everyone believes that their reality is the one and only one going on, so must I. Good luck to us all. Opinions are like belly buttons: everyone's got one. Now, on to the opening line, a make it or break it attempt to capture your attention without sounding precocious.

<u>Chapter One: Looney Tunes?</u>

"Every man at the bottom of his heart believes that he is a born detective." –John Buchan

It was the best of lines, it was the worst of lines. Rambling thoughts, poetry, bits and pieces of this and that, love and lust in who-dunnit sauce. Yum. If you don't get it, that's OK as well. Onward. Most everything that happens in this story takes place in Bizerkley: code name for Berkeley, California and nearby Palo Alto, home to Stanford University. I call my hometown Bizerkley because I was born in the time when it wasn't unusual to see a rainbow-attired guy holding a tie-dyed infant, getting into a rainbow-painted Volkswagen Bug. If any new idea ever needed fertile ground to grow, Bizerkley could provide.

Joe Freedom's my name and I'm a dick. A P.I. A cyber-sleuth. An investigator, finder of things, of information and occasional misplaced folks. This gig, my organization, interfaces with the worldly world through my website called 'Freedom Investigations.' The twenty-first century has been around just a bit more than a decade. I work out of my cyberspace lair using an avatar to make initial contact with potential clients. My avatar/alter ego looks like a cross between a film noire lady killer and a graphic novel superhero. Lots of muscles and mystery, that's my cyberself. Needless to say, I am constantly bombarded by nut cases. Looney Tune techno-geeks. People who do not leave their mom and pop's basement.

I was planning to make my career in rap music but the money hasn't exactly been rolling in. Luckily, I have a 'license to investigate' that I can fall back on. That also has yet to have me rolling in dough, financially stable, or able to pay rent. Occasionally I'll get a case, the money paying kind. I usually have to 'come up with the goods' before I earn any more than a retainer. I can boast of a 60/40 percent success rate. You pick the side that represents me.

My most unusual case is going to be filed under the name Huckleberry Dick. That's the cybermoniker of my most recent and only paying client. Still, a $200 retainer and promise of a $grand$ is sufficient motivation to get me to leave my Man Cave, my Mom and Pop's basement. I call my mom Mother Freedom and my father, Byll.

Our family home looks identically different from every other up-scale dwelling on our block. Money lives here. Dad, the pudgy patriarch of the family brought home the big bacon by transforming old newspapers into new news as a chemical engineer. That's why he could afford a two-story bungalow with basement when he put ten grand down in the early '80s. Mom maintained my original bedroom just like I left it when I left to marry my biggest mistake.

I am not basement bound. I am free to come and go as I please. But why? My studio apartment/recording studio/room/Man Cave, has many creature comforts, privacy, and my recording equipment. Unfortunately, my plans to be a mega-famous white rapper are in the crapper. I've got some good tunes but not a clue about promotion. I'd have money and a place of my own, but I gave it all to my first wife in return for my sanity which is now in question. In the divorce settlement I gave her pretty much everything I'd acquired in the way of assets in all my thirty-three years on the planet. All I asked in return was that she not live with me, talk to me or in any other way continue to drive me crazy.

I may not be clinically depressed but I'm obviously bummed out about the situation that is my life. I've heard suffering can be a good thing for an artist. Whoop-dee-do. People are starting to notice my lack of interaction with others unless they are anonymous cybertypes like myself. My parents threatened eviction if I don't see a therapist so I have left the basement on two occasions since starting on my great American rap album. I keep a cyberjournal with my writings and secret recordings of my sessions with Doctor Vana Fox in a cloud. The first session with its poetic preface is as follows.

Let me lay it down for you
    It's what I had to do
        And wouldn't you
            If most folks said you were crazy?

I just had to know on the down low
    Went to see a shrink, yo
        Hoping she'd just say I'm lazy

Not to say depressed
    As you might have guessed
        From times I just sit and mope

It could be psychosis
    Or neural neurosis
        But she went and blamed it on dope

Now I never lied
    We're all a little bit fried
        But I think what I think when I wanna

I get things done
    And sure, I have fun
        But a guy's gonna do
            what he's gonna

Chapter Two: Session One Recording

Her "office" is outdoors in summer sun with large canvas umbrellas and a couch/lounge chair suspended from the beams of an overhead trellis sporting bougainvillea blossoms and thorns. The 'couch' is for me and the Doc sits near a small glass table on pillows covering the outdoor deck's built-in benches. I don't know what happens if it rains. With the drought we've been having, I'd probably dance a jig if it did rain. I like to think she'd dance too.

Vana: Come and make yourself comfortable.

Joe: Nice office.

Vana: Thanks. I try. I see from your application for treatment that you're a performer.

Joe: I break it down, some.

Vana: And that means…?

Joe: I rap.

Vana: I see. A poet.

Joe: A rapper, slam poet, man poet, understand though it feels whack to you, I'll get back to you after taking it 'round, shaking it down to be about sound and rhythm which is time wrapped around rhyme, marinated in metaphor, have we met before? Been there before but back to you and what you do or will do with me. It could be crazy.

Vana: Yes, crazy. You mentioned in your reason for coming here that your family and friends think you are…

Joe: Crazy.

Vana: Not engaging life as you used to.

Joe: Checked out, so to speak.

Vana: Tell me about that.

Joe: I see nothing wrong with vegging out. Some days it's not worth chewing through the restraints.

Vana: You weren't answering your phone.

Joe: I wasn't all there. Had nothing to say.

Vana: Sounds like you may have been depressed.

Joe: It's relative. I can handle my thoughts. And distract them when I can't.

Vana: How do you do that?

Joe: Some TV. Some internet. Recording. Some good smoke or a good book.

Vana: What do you read?

Joe: Mysteries mostly. Life needs more mystery.

Vana: Well, we'll see if we can unravel the mystery that is you in the next few weeks. We'll be meeting once a week. Will Thursdays work out for you?

Joe: My schedule is free.

Vana: Good.

Joe: Do I call you Doc, Doc?

Vana: Ms. Fox works for me.

Joe: OK, Doc. So how's this work?

Vana: You tell me about yourself and I listen. Then, if the situation calls for it, I can offer some alternatives.

Joe: Straighten me out.

Vana: Help you to function better, whatever that means to you.

Joe: I get to decide.

Vana: It's your life.

Joe: I like that.

Vana: Alright, let's get started.

Joe: And though we talked for about a half hour more

All I remember are her eyes

Eyes I could dive into and come up refreshed

She was good lookin' and always lookin' at me

But not intrusive

More illusive

Or inclusive

Taking me into a dream

With her eyes alone

Like they shone

With a light of their own

But I ain't fallin' for no qwack yo

      That would be whack you know

But I realize

It's more than just her eyes

      So I am definitely going back

<u>Chapter Three: Where She Be</u>

The e-mail missive arrived, as most do, while I wasn't looking. More likely sleeping. Possibly eating. It doesn't really matter when it arrived, only that it was there and I finally checked my mail. It seemed legit but the name on the return e-mail address was strange: huckleberrydick@stanford.edu

Turns out Huckleberry Dick was in reality a professor of American Literature at Stanford University: one Dr. Otis Grille. His daughter was 'missing' and he was hoping 'Freedom Investigations' could find some way to contact her; find her and put her father's worries to rest. At least I'm going to be getting out of my Man Cave after months of high-burn-nation. I hadn't gone out since my last meeting with Dr. Fox that took place on her family deck in morning sun:

Vana: It's good to see you. I wasn't sure you'd show.

Joe: Why?

Vana: You seemed…distracted and a bit secretive.

Joe: We've all got our secrets.

Vana: But I want you to feel comfortable in sharing anything with me. I can't help you if you're not open and honest.

Joe: I guess I have issues with 'Open.' Seems I get in the most trouble when I 'open' my mouth and say what I think is true.

Vana: When you're brutally honest?

Joe: Socially inept. I piss people off. And most people don't really wanna hear the truth. They like everything safe and superficial.

Vana: And you?

Joe: I like to stir the pot. Goof on people. Put them through their paces. It's how I play.

Vana: Would you say you're manipulative?

Joe: Let's just say, even when I'm aware of my actions or the possible consequences, it doesn't seem to stop me from saying or doing most anything that comes to mind. I'm an excitement junky. I don't hold back.

Vana: Well, that should make our sessions fun.

Joe: I can be polite when I want to.

Vana: No, I insist. I want you to feel free to say whatever you want.

Joe: You're a fox, Fox.

Vana: Except that.

Joe: See?

Vana: I believe in keeping things professional. It's the only way I can help you.

Joe: There's more than one way to skin a cat.

Vana: Let's concentrate on your relationships with others, today. You suggested that you may have some trouble interacting with others.

Joe: It's their trip. I'm cool with that. Let the chips fall where they may. I just calls 'em as I sees 'em.

Vana: Give me an example.

Joe: Say some guy is all full of himself, thinks he knows everything about everything. I just point out what's going on as I see it.

Vana: And he takes offense…

Joe: If he takes a swing at me which is both _offensive_ and offensive, I try to make sure he misses me. Two years of aikido in Junior High. I'm a lover, not a fighter.

Vana: So, you're not afraid to be honest in conversation, even if it leads to trouble.

Joe: I like to think so.

Vana: I bet you do. And honesty is a good thing. Tact is something else. It all depends on what kind of result you're looking for.

Joe: Just keeping things interesting.

Vana: 'Excitement Junky', I believe were your words for it.

Joe: You do listen.

Vana: Oh, I hear you…

Joe: And that's a bit exciting. To be around someone who can see through me. No place to hide.

Vana: Let's hope that's a positive thing.

Joe: Positively.

Vana: Let's get back to relationships. Do you get along better with men or with women?

Joe: Are you asking whether I'm straight or gay? Look in my eyes.

Vana: Your flirtatious nature betrays you.   I was referring to friendships.

Joe: I have friends of all persuasions. They put up with my bullshit and I return the favor.

Vana: Can you clarify your 'bullshit?'

Joe: Like liking to be honest. You know, honesty bullshit. If you can't stand the heat, step away from the fire, mi amigo.

Vana: Lie to me.

Joe: What?

Vana: I just want to see if you can.

Joe: I think…you're….boring.

Vana: Nope, you're not very good at it.

Joe: Told you.

> And I told her stuff
>   I'd been hiding
>   even from myself
>   'cause I wanted it to work
>   Wanted her to know me
>   To see if she'd run away
>   Or keep looking at me with those
>   'deer in the headlights' eyes
>
>   Didn't realize she
>   could get all inside my head
>   Like opening up a can of
>   alphabet soup
>   And pouring my story into a bowl
>   for me to see

Roll with it and it might set me free?
Is anything I say really me?
Or just a game I so love to play
To play at love only
Once burned I've learned where love can lead
Why do I need to walk on eggshells around her?

Not wanting to break this beginning

Will it break me
when she takes me
to places I don't wanna see?

I reach out
Wanting to climb aboard her life raft

It's all stormy seas

(oh, please home boy)

I know it's whack
but I'm going back
for session three.

Chapter Four: On the Case

I spent the early morning hours, my most coherent time of day, researching Dr. Otis Grille (yes, he could afford to pay) and his daughter, Alex. I become one with my computer. I figure if I'm ever on life support, unplug me, then plug me back in and see if that helps. I had no need to access big data via a cloud or conduct a query; the university website gave plenty of info on all its teaching staff.   Grille has degrees from Ohio Wesleyan and Princeton in literature. His doctorate credentials allowed him to teach American Lit at any institute of higher learning. I assume he chose Stanford to be close to Alexandra. She was in her second year there when Otis left Princeton for California's sunnier climes. His DMV photo showed a man of sixty years with Einstein hair and a mischievous smile. He was looking right into the camera as if participating in a conversation.

Alexandra was more of a mystery. I wasn't finding diddly squat about her through social media. I had hoped she would be on Facebook where most internet idiots willingly display the most intimate details of their lives including selfies (photos), relationship status and oh-so-important opinions. She wasn't there. I couldn't access her friends list to find people to interview about her because she didn't play the social media game. She wasn't listed with any phone companies so a GPS search was out. If she had a phone, she purchased the plan using another name. Was she a spy?

Through school records I was able to ascertain (find out) that she had done well academically in school, but didn't belong to any clubs, participated in no sports, rarely even attended a fieldtrip. The thing I found most odd was that there were no photos of her in the school yearbook for any of the time she spent at Sterling Academy, a private/expensive boarding school/country club. Her father had paid through the nose for that one, even taking out a second mortgage to ensure he could cover the cost for four years. If Alexandra hadn't gotten a partial scholarship to Stanford, Dr. Grille would have had to consider filing for bankruptcy.

I found out Alex rents a cozy cottage a block from Fraternity Row and shares expenses with her roommate who she met through a Beginning Literature class, Stacey Hodges. I am currently conducting a stake out of that cozy cottage in hopes of talking with Stacey when she returns from classes. Maybe she could shed some light on where Alex has gone. Disappeared. Run off. Where and why?

I've come prepared with a backpack stuffed with granola bars and several liters of water. I'd been waiting three granola bars already and the liter of water is wreaking havoc on my bladder. I've been thumbing through a hand-bound manuscript with Alex's name on the cover. I found it crammed between text books on Psychology, Art and Philosophy on a shelf in her bedroom. OK, so I admit I took a peek inside her house which some might call breaking and entering but I didn't have to break anything when I found that open window. I know it must have been Alex's room and not Stacey's because the walls were plastered with all kinds of art and Alex is an Art major.

But back to this manuscript with Alex's name on it. There are typed pages and hand written notes and honestly, it's got some pretty twisted stuff in it. I have no way of knowing if it is the least bit 'autobiographical' and could give insight into the young woman I am so painstakingly seeking in hopes of a paycheck. For what it's worth, here's what the manuscript says:

Somebody wake me, I must be dreaming, thought Marci
melting into Ian in the afterglow of what surely must be love,
nuzzling her nose into the soft sweat scent of his tussled,
auburn hair

For Ian and only Ian,
she would write love poems and hide them in his pockets
like Christmas presents.

Poems like:

> *If every atom of our world*
> > *in time be torn apart*
> *I would not cry*
> > *Nor could I die*
> *Because you hold my heart*

She wanted to wrap all her dreams around him like a cozy cotton- comforter,
> *warmed by his intense heat.*
Oh, the way he could stir to fire her passion's flame.

Marci: Ian, I think you missed a spot. You promised to lick me all over.
> *Well, I'm waiting. I'm wanting.*

Can love be made?

> *in her bed*
> > *on blankets of leaves*
> > > *on roof tops*

Did they create it?
Or share it?
Can love be possessed?

Standing on mountains at sunset
Painted by campfires and moonlight

Dipping thirsty hands into a lake of love?

He would take his time.

Stare at her
her eyes
her skin
every feature and curve

move his lips across her body so close they would brush against-   the fine hair of her

        and make her tingle

              giggle and purr

        suck in air through clenched teeth

              to moan

                    to sigh

                        to beg for more with outstretched fingers

But how did it all begin?

By chance or fate?

Destiny or design?

With tires screeching on polished concrete, Ian McVain guides his black Porsche Boxter into a space at the university parking complex. Having cruised around the campus, it is clear to him that this is the happy hunting ground for fresh flesh for his talent/modeling agency, "Seeing Stars."

Now he must take to the sidewalks, malls and hallways, handing out business cards for every feminine form that fits his fancy and fantasies. Guys get cards too, but only to appear professional if there are ladies present.

Ian runs a talent/modeling agency which is a front for a porn studio.

The young women are told to call and set up appointments for auditions, then asked to attend a preliminary photo shoot, bringing along three outfits and a bathing suit to strut their stuff.

They'll be video taped reading lines of all kinds: sales slogans, character voice-overs, even a little Shakespeare and asked to convey a variety of emotions, from mourning to moaning, tears to terror.

They'll be required to take in-house acting classes, yoga, Pilates, martial arts, swimming and dance lessons. They pay big bucks for head shots and resumes.

After a few months, the spunky ones will be asked how they feel about nude modeling and the less inhibited will be offered "cameos" in adult films with some of McVain's many partnerships.

Some will be offered modeling and dancing tours in Japan and end up working in hostess bars. Sex sells, and Ian likes money. Money can't buy love, but what Ian wants only looks like love. It's not about caring and sharing. He doesn't play well with others. It's all about pleasure; all about him.

The brunette who liked being tied to the bed and begged Ian to drip hot wax across her breasts.

The leggy, bleach-bottle blond with black roots showing, who always wanted to be taken from behind.

The red head whose pubes proved that was her natural color. She wouldn't let him in her vagina but would let him rub the tip of his cock against her willingly wet labia until he would explode.

He rarely remembered their names. They were merely a means to an end. It seemed the only reason he had a heart was to pump blood into his penis.

After a few hours of pounding the college pavement, McVain needed to get out of the sun and find him some food. On his way to the Campus Center food court, he saw her.

She was lying half in sun and half in shade under a tree on- a sloping hill, lost in a book,
sipping a fruit smoothie and looking…delicious.

Short cropped black hair,

big eyes,

thin,

hint of gothic,

very lovely.

He thinks: I must have her.

He plans his seduction carefully.

McVain sat down on the grass, under a tree, about three trees away from where she lay, reading, studying, alternating between sun and shade, and he composed a poem for this nameless coed who had caught his fancy, hoping a literary approach would be the right one. Then he crumpled up the paper, and with the skill of a basketball superstar at the free throw line, lobed his missive in her direction. It rolled to within inches of the text book she was struggling to concentrate on. She picked it up and looked to see where it had come from and saw Ian's smile for the first time. She unfolded it and read.

Never forget

no matter how tall you've grown

that you began life's journey as a babe

who couldn't have survived alone.

And though you speak in learned circles

with the knowledge of your years

your first utterances were babble

punctuated by tears.

No matter how self sufficient you feel

or what others may have told you,

just as in your beginning

you still need someone to hold you.

Let me be that someone.

She was a sucker for poetry.

*That poem was the first of many he used to melt her heart
        and find his way between her thighs.*

He walked over, smiling that Ian smile.

Marci: So you need a hug, do you? Sounds kind of needy.

Ian: On the contrary. I have so much to give.

Marci: Such as?

Ian: Love. Some call it love.

Marci: Love that burns too hot consumes itself. I just wish…

Ian: No. Don't wish.

Don't wish upon a falling star

Or set your hopes on a heaven far

Your love's the key to paradise

Let me in
    Let love suffice.

Ian, quite unlike Ian, doesn't have sex with Marci
    the first time she makes it clear it could happen.

Maybe he likes the waiting.
    The wanting.

One day, he was late for their dinner date. Ian was entertaining an older woman with a big bank account and bigger tits. She had no idea. While she waited she wrote this for him:

I would be happy…no
    Cheerful…no
        Delighted to have you by my side

But you're not here
    You're absent
        You're missing

I eagerly await your arrival
    Your entrance
        Your appearance

But I'm fearfully afraid that you may not show at all
    And then you'll never see my loving loyalty
        And dedicated devotion

And I would be hurt…
    No, wounded …
        No, broken…hearted.

It was a Sunday.
She could have been in church
Instead she was in Ian's arms, again.
Again and again.
Willing and wanting and laughing and loving.
And it begins.
She stops giggling
He keeps staring into her eyes
Inches apart sharing breath
Warm fertile breath
Deep breaths that warn of exercise to come
Fight or flight darlin' and we are gonna fly
And she's on him
And he holds her up
And he's in her growing stronger, harder
And she moves
And he lets her
And he moves
And she wants him to move harder
And more
And deeper
And these tears will not stain you
Don't stop
I can't hesitate to love you
Won't stop and animals don't know love
I'm so close
You need this badly
Now! Hold me. Hold still. Just still. Just until I can take it all in.

    Ian would lie next to her, watching her sleep, listening to the rhythm of her breathing, composing poetry of apology is his head:

Me, the manipulator
I begin to see it
Rarely control it
Often deny it
Haven't perfected it
Wish I could stop it

Doubt that I need it
Enjoy when I do it
Know where I learned it
Know why I use it
Maybe I should quit.

Bullshit.
Ian screws anyone and everyone.
Ian is a walking STD, the gift that keeps on giving.
He plays the real gentleman
Until he loses interest
and Marci notices it hurts to piss

He drops her and is pretty cold about it.
Ian: I think we need to see other people.

Marci: Oh can't you be more original than that? Why don't you tell me you have an incurable disease and plan to run off to Egypt to dry up with the mummies?

Ian: I didn't mean to hurt you.

Marci: Well that's what love does when you take it away, Ian. Hurts like hell. Be honest with me. Is there someone else?

Ian: It's not that.

Marci: Then what is it, Ian? Do I bore you? Aren't I enough for you? Haven't I done everything you ever wanted?

Ian: I've got to go.

Marci: Then don't come back.

He leaves.

Marci: Don't you ever come back.

He leaves.

That awful week. That "had a love but that's gone now" awful aching week. That week, the university health clinic calls to inform Marci she has multiple STD's.

What did Ian say when they first met? "I've got so much to give" or some such bullshit.

That night, after taking her medications, Marci burns all of Ian's pictures. The inner Marci seethes, silently saying, "Call it stalking if you like motherfucker but I'm gonna follow you, gonna know your game. You ain't seen a woman scorned 'til you've got one hunting you."

You gotta do your research, that's one thing college taught Marci. It's a shame it couldn't teach her to be more discerning in her choice of men.

With a tip from a bouncer friend of a friend
She follows him
Dressed in a slutty hooker disguise
Marci keeps a distance
Watching
As Ian works the sex club movie room

Pillow talk he likes to call it

Pick your pleasure

And in a darkened corner
On satin pillows
Ian accepts an enema and
Body oil poured between his buttocks
A muffled mixture of cries both pain and pleasure
fingers caress moist lips
all lips at once then
loud slapping sounds on bare flesh

to the beat of the techno music mania

If you come on my tummy how can I swallow your children?

Then Ian is on to the group thing

And Marci must mix in to fit in

A tiled room for easy wash down

all aboard the train

You hold this…

You lick this

He takes a model (maybe movie starlet) from behind

Ian loves to organize

Marci has seen enough and doesn't want to be seen
so before things go any further
she is grabbing her g-string
and hitting the showers
and tossing her cookies
and madder than hell
And it is in anger that awful things are conceived.

Who would believe?
Marci seems like such a down-to-earth kind of girl, if a bit gothic.

     Allison is another story. Marci's best friend and confident knew all about Ian and the heartbreak (not to mention, infection) he caused. She saw things as black and white, good or bad, on God's Side or Devil be damned. And she had it in for Ian. She wanted his head (any one will do) on a platter.

Allison: We could frame him for rape.

Marci: I wouldn't want him near me.

Allison: I'll do it. I'll tie the bastard to the bed. Promise to lick his crack if I have to, then I jerk him off to get his semen on the sheets.

Marci: You've seen too many CSI shows…

Allison: Maybe while I've got him tied up, I'll have to hurt him a little. Maybe hurt him a lot.

Marci: Oh, could you? Would you? Just for me? And let me see.

Allison: Oh, you'll be hiding in the closet.

Marci: But can we do this?

Allison: Honey, if you'd only seen some of the looks that guy gave me when you weren't lookin'…I can get him in bed, or die trying.

And so it began

Two women with a plan

And the plot thickened

With Marci's suggestions and Allison's agreement

A plot not sealed in blood

But full of it

Blood red and hot and flowing and no stopping it until it all seemed so easy

Allison pretended to audition for his modeling agency, making it clear they could take things further, should take things to her place over champagne and strawberries.

Ian knew Allison was Marci's friend but was egotistical enough to think that she couldn't resist him, that she wouldn't harbor any ulterior motives, and she had a nice tight ass. It was settled. He'd buy the champagne.

Allison: I feel like such a bad girl. I mean, you were with Marci just a while ago.

Ian: Let's not worry about her. I want to know about you. All about you. Everything there is to know. If you know what I mean?

Allison: Oh, yea. You radiate it. What can I say? I like to party. Like to play. I'm theatrical. I always wanted to have a man at my mercy. Make him beg for it. Know what I mean?

Ian: Handcuffs, that sort of thing?

Allison: I'm all out of handcuffs. But I could tie you to the bed. I collect scarves for just such an occasion.

Ian: But then I can't hold you.

Allison: There will be time for that, now lie back, no, leave your clothes on. I will dispense with them later. Right hand first. I'm no girl scout but I know my knots. Now your left. That's not too tight, is it? Now for your feet. I don't want you squirming around while I work my magic. There, that's your left leg, now which leg wants my attention next?

Ian: That would be my third leg.

Allison: Well. We better make sure he roams free. Now just put your right leg, right up here. My, what strong thighs you have. This is going to be fun.

Ian: You're killing me.

Alison: Not quite. Not really. They say some things are worse than death.

Ian: You don't scare me.

Allison: But this might.

Ian: What is that? Some kind of super vibrator?

Alison: Ian, meet Taser.

And she zapped him in the thigh near his groin, Ian's body arching up like he was auditioning for the arc de triumph, his erection a lightning rod at the summit.

Then Marci came out of the closet (no gay reference intended) and the look on Ian's face went from pained to terrified. She had a look in her eyes he had never seen before in all their moments of intimacy. This was a look reserved for those who hurt children or hurt the child inside every woman.

Allison handed her the taser.

Marci: Where do you want it, Ian? You once asked me to kiss you all over. Have I missed a spot? I could test your testicles for you. See if they light up like Christmas lights. You believe in Christmas, don't you Ian, believe in gifts that keep on giving…

Ian: Marci, don't…

Marci: But I must…if only to shut you up.

And Marci applied the taser to the base of Ian's neck where she had once left a hickie, her badge of honor she called it. He shook and moaned and then collapsed and was silent.

Allison: Now we kill him?

Marci: A fate worse than death.

Allison: I say fuck the disinfectant. Just cut him.

Marci: No, we do it right. I want him to live. I want him to live without wanting, without wanting anyone ever again. Give him the tequila tourniquet.

Allison poured a mix of tequila and ludes down Ian's throat nearly choking him.

Marci: Don't drown him. He's mine. Or should I say they're mine.

And Marci made an incision just as her Uncle Walter had taught her with the young bulls on the farm come castratin' time. The incision was away from major veins so it wouldn't bleed much and she just squeezed. Squeezed first one and then the other testicle until they popped out of the scrotum to be snipped free. Forever free.

Marci: No need sew him up. Let him bleed a little. I sure did.

Allison: We could finish him.

Marci: No. No, this will kill him…more.

Marci washed her hands and before they left him there sprawled on Allison's bed, Marci leaned over to Ian's unhearing ear and whispered, "Game over, Ian. You may have held my heart, but I've got your balls."

They left him tied like fish jerky drying in the sun. He would be found five hours later due to an anonymous tip and would not die, though he would wish he had.

End

OMG. Is 'Marci' Alexandra's avatar? Could this have actually happened? Is this why she disappeared and if so, will she want to be found? It can't be real, can it?

I thought about asking Vana her opinion on the manuscript. Besides, it'll give me something more to talk about than just me. I'm running out of material.

I spent the next few days in cyberspace, trying to catch a scent of Alex's trail. As my next session with Vana approached, I noticed I'm finding it harder and harder to concentrate. There's just something healing about being with The Doc.

<u>Chapter Five: I Just Like Yelling</u>

It's breezy on Doc's deck but the umbrellas seem sufficiently anchored down and I find I'm calmed by the sound of the wind through the bougainvillea. She's wearing a tennis dress with, let me guess, just a bit more cleavage showing than my last visit and soon my calm dissipates as I contemplate what could be.

Vana: You realize everything you say to me is confidential.

Joe: I'm not gonna tell my friends or anything.

Vana: Do you have many friends?

Joe: What kind of whack question is that? I know people.

Vana: Friends you associate with…

Joe: Just the other day, my buddy Jules called me to bail him out after his chick said he was abusin' her. He never touched her.

Vana: Friends. People who like you, not who look to you to bail them out.

Joe: Why do I gotta be liked? You got some kind of hang up about that, huh?

Vana: We're not here to talk about me.

Joe: It's all about you. You come up with the questions and wanna know who associates with who. Everyone's got a bias they can't run from.

Vana: Are you running away from something?

Joe: There ya go, turnin' everything around!

Vana: Does that upset you?

Joe: I just like yelling. You, however, are in love with the sound of your own voice.

Vana: We're not talking about me.

Joe: That's funny, I was.

Vana: So you'd like to be the shrink now?

Joe: I'd like your salary. And yeah, I think I could straighten you out given half a chance.

Vana: Straighten me out? Like I need fixing?

Joe: We all have our rough edges. That's what friends are for, to round off your rough edges.

Vana: So we're friends now?

Joe: Could be. It's a two-way street. Besides, the better the relationship with the therapist, the more likely the success.

Vana: I'm a loss for words.

Joe: And how does that make you feel?

Vana: Stop that.

Joe: You do it.

Vana: I'm supposed to. It's what I do. And you're the one paying the bill, or your insurance is. Somebody's gotta pay.

Joe: Oh, it costs ya. Now, let's begin at the beginning. How was your childhood?

Vana: I was going to ask you the same thing.

Joe: You first.

Vana: It was fine, obviously.

Joe: Obviously. Mine was sweet. Loving parents, small towns and wild women.

Vana: What makes them, 'wild'?

Joe: If you don't know by now…

Vana: Don't even go there.

Joe: A full sexual history seems called for. It could prove enlightening.

Vana: Now that sounds like a shrink.

Joe: Imitation is the sincerest form of flattery.

Vana: You flatter me.

Joe: I'll try anything.

Vana: To do what?

Joe: Make a new friend. You asked if I had any friends. No time like now.

Vana: I thought you were flirting.

Joe: That would be unprofessional.

Vana: You're not getting paid.

Joe: Who needs money?
Vana: Don't you?

Joe: I'm giving it all to you.

Vana: Well, good.

Joe: Now we're getting somewhere.

Vana: How can you tell?

Joe: You're smiling.

Vana: Was not and can't make me.

Joe: In touch with the child in you.

Vana: Everyone likes to play. You're playing with me now.
I can tell

Joe: As long as everyone wins.

Vana: How do you feel about women?

Joe: I get to ask the questions.

Vana: You're avoiding answering.

Joe: Let's change the subject. Women are too confusing to analyze.

Vana: You wanted to be the shrink.

Joe: And how does that make you feel?

Vana: I feel fine.

Joe: I bet you do.

Vana: That was suggestive.

Joe: But not a suggestion. However, everything that happens here is confidential.

Vana: I hope so, doctor.

Joe: Ever play doctor?

Vana: Can't say. Doctor patient confidentiality.

Joe: Two points.

Vana: Oh, I'm way ahead of you.

Joe: Read me like a book, huh? How many serious relationships have you had?

Vana: I wouldn't…

Joe: Be serious?

Vana: Tell you.

Joe: You're being defensive. Good. We must be getting somewhere, touching on some hot spots. We'll get to the bottom of this. And I'm not being suggestive…however nice that bottom may be.

Vana: Some people have to hit bottom before they seek help.

Joe: Now <u>you're</u> being suggestive. I like that. OK, let's review: childhood; check, dating; you won't tell me, confidentiality; noted, progress; definitely.

Vana: How does that make <u>you</u> feel?

Joe: Helpful. Concerned. Pensive. Intrigued.

Vana: Are those your true feelings or just your spelling words for this week?
Joe: The child in me recognizes the child in you and reminds you that my dad can beat up your dad. And, yes, I have feelings, all the time, but we're not hear to talk about me.
Vana: Yes, it's all about me. Well, doctor, my mother worries over me too much and my father was never demonstrative.

Joe: He never demonstrated?

Vana: He was reluctant to show affection. Not his style. And you?

Joe: I'm very affectionate.

Vana: I meant your relationship with your parents.

Joe: They're not huggy kissy types. I love them and vice my versa. They're salt of the earth, Protestant, Republicans. I guess that's why I'm a Democrat.

Vana: Who knows why anybody is anything

Joe: That's traitorous talk for a shrink. You're supposed to know why people are the way they are and do what they damn well do.

Vana: Every time we come up with a theory to explain it all, someone goes and does something surprising.

Joe: You surprise me.

Vana: You're flirting again. It'll never work.

Joe: It shouldn't feel like work.

Vana: I like to work. I'm a pro.

Joe: I love the way you say that.

Vana: One track mind.
Joe: I don't mind.

Vana: Obviously.

Joe: Obsessively.

Vana: I've noticed.

Joe: You should write that down in your notes.

Vana: I keep it all up here.

Joe: You should see what I've got going 'up here.' It's crazy.

Vana: That's why we're here. 'Crazy'. How does that feel?

Joe: Like they say, "Six out of seven dwarfs aren't Happy". I feel weird. Worried and weird. Worried, weird, and sometimes wired.

Vana: An alliteration conversation."

Joe: Oh, you're good.

Vana: So I'm told.

Joe: Now, you're flirting.

Vana: Was not.

Joe: Bragging then. That really hurts.

Vana: How?

Joe: It hurts when you're so close to something so good…and then…

Vana: Oh, the time. We'll have to schedule another session. You know, you put the fun is 'dys'fun'ctual.'

Joe: Schedule me immediately. Dinner?

Vana: Next week, Thursday. Same time. You can play doctor.

Joe: Before I go, I wanted to show you this. It's a manuscript by a missing person I've been hired to find. I was hoping you'd read it and let me know if there's any truth to this fiction.

Vana: I'll look it over, but I'd probably need more information about this person to make more than a guess.

        Yes! Now I had more I could talk to her about than my sorry ass self.

        I stopped worrying about being nuts and just filled my head with thoughts of her.

I went through countless imaginary sessions in my head

        Several of them ended up with both of us on the couch.

Maybe she was playing me
         Like a bluesy saxophone

         Making me hope
                  When I'm hopeless
                  Can't cope unless
         There's more of her
     In my moments ahead

                  There I said it
         I'm not proud
     I'd shout it out loud
         If that's what it takes
              And all my mistakes
                  Are worth the blood and bruises
         If they have brought me here
Created this situation
         Wrapped it up in expectation and fear

         But she's here
              On the same planet

                       Breathing the same air as me
                  I, the captured free
              Hoping for 'we'
     We this
              We that
              We lovers' spat
                  We tit for tat
                       We, I tried that
                       We sit and chat

We share
     Compare
         I walk on air
              Around her

     Found her looking for myself

<u>Chapter Six: Stacy Space Case</u>

"A lot of girls think they have to choose between being the smart geeky type or the beautiful bimbo." –Danica McKellar

I hadn't done a stake-out since the last time when Stacey didn't show. There I was in my inconspicuous Volvo station wagon, vintage '91, parked not far from Fraternity Row. I could hear the sounds of testosterone talking from several hundred yards away; bad boys in rutting season and it's always that season when one is twenty going on eighteen. Alex and Stacey's rental had the run down look of student housing where no one takes responsibility for the yard and nature is free to grow with abandon. The street was quiet, not a lick of traffic and then…

It wasn't hard to see her coming. Stacy is the kind of girl guys don't mind watching under any circumstances. Coming. Going. Young. Beyond pretty but a bit too smiley. She had bounce in her walk, a blond ponytail swinging kind of sashay-like that says, "I know you're watching and this is for you." If I didn't have the hots for Doctor Darling, I'd say Stacey would make a plausible 'Plan B'.

I got out of the car, my wallet in hand for official flashing of credentials as I did my best to sound professional. "Stacey Hodges?" "Who wants to know?" "Joe Freedom, private investigations. I've been hired to find Alexandra Grille."

Stacey: I don't care if you're Captain America. I don't trust strangers and I don't speak to PI's.

Joe: She's missing.

Stacey: Dur. Her dad's only called about a thousand times.

Joe: When was the last time you saw her?

Stacey: Not talking.

Joe: Can you think of anyone who might harm her?

Stacey: Quit following me.

Joe: May I come in?

Stacey: No, you can piss off.

Joe: I need to find her.

Stacey: Not my problem. Let go of my door.

Joe: What if she's in trouble?

Stacey: She'd love it.

 Joe: What does that mean?

Stacey: If I explain, will you leave me alone?

Joe: I promise.

Stacey: She thinks of herself as some kind of artist, but the only thing she's good at is stirring up trouble. She's a chaos-loving drama queen. Now, are we through?

Joe: Not just yet…

Stacey: You promised.

Joe: Was she seeing anyone?

Stacey: Yeah, but I never met him. I think it was a "him." I'm into "hims." (flirty smile)

Joe: Did she mention a name?

Stacey: No. That's why I can't be sure. But she said the sex was great.

Joe: She told you that?

Stacey: Guys just don't get girl talk, do they? She said she was having a great time. No, that wasn't the word: she said it was 'an adventure'. That sounds great to me, even if it was weird.

Joe: She said, "Weird"?

Stacey: Yeah, but she didn't explain. Just gave me the look. You know, the look.

Joe: Was she acting weird or different?

Stacey: That's what she does. Avant-Garde is just French for fucking crazy. She missed classes, partied too much, disappeared for days at a time.

Joe: But this time she stayed gone. How long has it been?

Stacey: A week or so. I only saw her as she was going out the door. She said something about a flash mob party somewhere on campus. I didn't ask for details 'cause I didn't want to go. I had to study for my Psych midterm.

Joe: There may still be e-mails about the flash mob on her computer. Is it OK if I take a look?

Stacey: Knock yourself out. Just let me be.

Joe: Deal.

A quick run through of Alex's net searches revealed little, though I did notice a cyberspace inquiry into drug rehabilitation centers: New Dawn Collective and Pathfinders Recovery Ranch. This might relate to what Stacey said about Alex "partying too much."

I can't tell if Alex has clicked on any sites for additional information, but it might be a good idea to look into local drug rehab centers. Wouldn't hurt to know where they are. (not for me, so stop dreaming)

I thanked Stacey for letting me "borrow" Alex's laptop (which I held onto like it was already mine) and noticed she had 'slipped into something more comfortable:' a loose fitting, thin muscle shirt, and I assume shorts but if she did have shorts, they were shorter than the shirt. All for show. All for me. But I like to think I know better so I made some excuse about following up other leads and let myself out. (Did I see her pout?) Temptation is just another word for college girls.

The things Stacey told me about Alex kept bouncing around inside my skull: parties too much, sometimes gone for days, a mysterious 'him,' adventurous sex. Things were getting interesting.

<u>Chapter Seven: Meet Chew In Da Middle</u>

"Reality is merely an illusion, albeit a very persistent one."

–Albert Einstein

On the way to the cozy 'office' Vana kept above her parents' garage, next to the family mansion, in a very upscale neighborhood, I got to singing country in the car, scat singin', keeping the beat on the steering wheel drum set, playing all the instruments, though not all at once. The Volvo's windows were down as in not blocking the sound of my singing:

Well, I'll meet you in the middle if you'll meet me at the end.

 I may not always love you but I'll always be your friend

and if you want some huggin,' you know just what to do.

You just call me honey and I'll be there with you

Ain't no time in the summer
	Ain't no time in the fall
		Ain't no time for much of anything
			Anything at all
But I'll make time,
	Honey, I'll make time,
		Honey, I'll sure make some time for you

			Honey it's a cryin' shame.
			You play me for a fool
				when you make our love a game.

Today it rained, sweet Lordy hallelujah, and that meant the sun deck was now the pool so we held session at Vana's kitchen table in her 'oh so neat' studio above her parents three car garage. I began analyzing my surroundings immediately. She had a compact kitchen and dining area with windows meeting at the room's corner. Good utilization of space worthy of even a Man Cave. Two doors led to what I guessed were the bathroom and her bedroom. Her bedroom. Would I ever see that inner sanctum? Would I ever.

Vana: You're early.

Joe: The clock's slow. Been slow all week.

Vana: No comment.

Joe: You feel it too?

Vana: Today we'll be talking about you.

Joe: You rhymed!

Vana: And this session is timed. Let's not waste it. I want to know more about your childhood.

Joe: It was good.

Vana: Details, si vous plais.

Joe: Anything. Just speak French again.

Vana: Vous avez le tete de poisson.

Joe: Which means?

Vana: You have the head of a fish.

Joe: Yes, I think we have a breakthrough. Conked the slimy cod on the noggin' and out comes scattered memories and moments…all inexplicable.

Vana: But it must be explained. I want to know…more about you.

Joe: Strictly professional, I suppose.

Vana: So be it. Now, growing up…

Joe: I did the regular kid stuff. I loved to take my bow and arrow and shoot straight up in the sky, then try not to be there when the arrow came down.

Vana: You like risk.

Joe: I take my chances. I like to experience it all.

Vana: Drugs?

Joe: No thanks, I'm driving.

Vana: You're willing to take risks with your mind. Your medical history list numerous substances.

Joe: If you don't experiment, you don't know.

Vana: Your drug of choice?

Joe: Pot mostly, but it's not my favorite high. I like hiking in open pasture on a mountain side.

Vana: A natural high?

Joe: Looking for shrooms. Magic.

Vana: Describe the feeling.

Joe: It's a trip. Imagine with me, walking down a mountain ridge, wild flowers and butterflies everywhere, and I got to thanking God, and telling him what an awesome job He did in making this world. Then I got to thinking about what Jesus said.

Vana: What did Jesus say to you?

Joe: I wasn't hearing voices. I mean, what he said in the Bible, you know, I stand at the door and knock. You open the door, I'll come in. So I said He could use my eyes to see how beautiful the morning was. Take my feet and walk and feel the earth again…and I felt filled with love for it all. Oh, give us this day our daily delusion. If that was nuts, then crazy it is. If that is my myth, I want more. "It's not what you look at that matters, it's what you see."

Vana: Did you just quote Thoreau?

Joe: I do read, you know.

Vana: Do you feel that love now, like you did that day?

Joe: Around the edges…when I get centered…when I remember.

Vana: You wanted to be like Jesus."

Joe: To be…or not to be…

Vana: Would you say you're religious?

Joe: Brought up Baptist, moved to Methodist and haven't been to church in a month of Sundays.

Vana: Why not?

Joe: It bores me. The world's my congregation and every day's Sunday.

Vana: Do you pray?

Joe: I start a lot of prayers but usually space out before I ever hit 'amen'. I'm a stream of consciousness kid. My thoughts flitter about like butterflies on amphetamines.
Vana: You're saying you have trouble concentrating?

Joe: When you're around.

Vana: That's enough to make a woman blush, kind sir, but let's keep your meandering mind on topic.

Joe: Which is?

Vana: Your childhood. You were brought up in the church, haven't been back, you like to commune with nature…

Joe: And get high.

Vana: Why high?

Joe: Maybe it's the mental challenge. Reality's easy, so why not try it with neurons a-blazin', brain-a-buzzin' and what interesting, if not unusual, things happen.

Vana: Unusual?

Joe: Yeah, not usual. Not the same ol' same ol'. Take it up a notch.

Vana: "You like to make things harder for yourself?"

Joe: I like a challenge, a game. I was made for play. I can play all day. If there are boundaries, I wanna push 'em. If there are rules, I wanna break 'em. If my bullshit alarm goes off, Captain Clueless wants to be ready to fight for freedom for all!

Vana: A rebel without a clue!

Joe: Now, let's talk about you.

Vana: Let's not.

Joe: Shut down, but not turned off.
Vana: Back to drugs…

Joe: Hip, hip, hooray.

Vana: You smoke weed, hike through pastures for cowpie fungi.

Joe: I'm a fun guy. (fungi)

Vana: What other drugs?

Joe: What you got?

Vana: I am not writing you a prescription for anything.

Joe: Why I'm down right disappointed in this here medical model. I was expectin' pill pushers with PhDs.

Vana: Would you admit you seem to have an addictive personality?

Joe: I could get used to coming here. I like it here. And I need your help. What's your professional take on that manuscript? Am I searching for a killer, a nutcase or both?

Vana: You mean, do I think the things in Alex's story actually happened? Not literally.

Joe: No?

Vana: I think the whole thing could just be a metaphor describing in hyperbole a failed relationship. Some guy broke her heart and she wishes she could cut off his nuts. A lot of women have felt that way.

Joe: But not you. Tell me it ain't so.

Then she threw me out before the scheduled time.
        That was getting to be a habit.
But she seemed to be smilin' or smirkin' the whole time she did it
        and damn if she didn't schedule me in for the next week.

I saw a Bible on her bookshelf as I was leaving her place and asked if she reads it and she replied, "Every damn day." Damn I like this girl.

I wonder if there's anything suggestively seductive in the Good Book?

I might need to re-read the Song of Solomon.

I want to impress her
I'm sure I undress her with my eyes
But it's her eyes that tantalize
Sure, I realize I must respect 'the process'
Still I continue to undress her
My confidential confessor
Professional boundaries about her
I am not right in my head without her

I know it's crazy
But crazy's what I do

Being nuts is starting to make sense

No mo freedom-jones
In these bare bones since I met her

This is nuts
This is perfect

This is costing me
I don't care cuz

I'm starting to care was
there ever a tale of more woe, than this libidinous Romeo?

Shakespeare be damned
Slack-jaw poetry slammed

I am the man laid low

Without a single blow to my ego

                        Oh, she go

            But can she see inside?
            Can she analyze?

Does she know what I fantasize?

That would be whack

Still I'm going back.

Chapter Eight: PI Pit Bull

Otis Grille taught two classes on Tuesdays (tough life, professor) but I was able to make an appointment to talk with him on an afternoon when he maintains 'office hours.' He said students rarely came in to see him except to beg for an extension when papers came due midterm and near the end of the semester. The semester has just started so the coast was clear. I told him I'd drop in around two.

I had four hours to kill and I can't eat lunch for more than an hour so I decided to check out some of the rehab facilities nearest to Stanford. There were two: Harmonic Transformations and Safe Place Meditative Services. After the usual run around, I was permitted to show the photo I had of Alex to some low level administrator who didn't fail to mention confidentiality issues but showed me by her lack of reaction to the photo that Alex was not among their clientele. I've learned to read most people fairly accurately, if you don't count women. Vana has me so tied up in knots I feel like a fishing net lodged in a coral reef. What a pain in the ass beautiful feeling love is.

Few folks know that Stanford has on display several works by the artist Rodin; the most famous being a statue of a seated, nude man resting his head on his hand: The Thinker. I too, though not nude, was sitting and doing some thinking; mostly about Vana, but also about the case, just not as much and let's face it, it's complicated. I just ended too many married years with 'Miss-Make-Me-Nuts' and now I've got those 'here I go again' crazy kind of thoughts when I should be following down leads but my thought train maintains constant locomotion with the notion that Doc Dear is ever so slowly coming around to my way of thinking. My thoughts are constantly in question depending upon who you ask: my shrink, my parents, my few friends. Now what was I thinking about? Oh, yeah, I've got remember to head over to the Professor's building and stay focused.

Dr. Grille's office door was open when I arrived. He invited me in, closing the door and locking it. His office was wall-to-wall book cases stuffed with the stuff of greatness; every piece of great literature that most folks were not going to read in this life time. The first words out of his mouth were, "Did you find out anything about my daughter?" I wasn't sure where to start. Should I mention what Stacey Space-case had said about weird sex? I mean, if I was a father, would I want to hear that?

Joe: I'm just starting the investigation. I interviewed her roommate and learned that she was seeing someone. Were you aware of her dating some guy?

Grille: I don't think so. I honestly feel like I need a translator every time I try to talk with her. My daughter finds significance in the strangest things. And she's adamant about Art with the religious fervor of a zealot when all I see is a lost child who used to need me.

Joe: I'm going to find her. If she doesn't want to be found, it'll take a little longer but I'll find her. That's what you pay me for.

Grille: I realize two hundred dollars isn't much of a retainer…

Joe: Don't worry, I'll bill you for gas money and incidentals as soon as I come up for air but for now let's focus on finding her. Did she ever discuss her drug use with you?

Grille: When she went through her graffiti art phase, I accused her of sniffing paint but I never saw any signs of a problem really. I was usually more focused on her outlook.

Joe: What about her outlook?

Grille: As she got older she became more fearless, like an adrenaline junky. She did things I would never think of doing: extreme sports, scuba diving, bungee jumping, kite surfing. She even jumped out of a perfectly good airplane wearing some special soaring suit. She said it was such a rush she almost forgot to deploy her chute.

Joe: Did that same spirit seem to apply to her relationships?

Grille: I don't know. I was never any good talking to her about boys and that sort of thing. She'd always pat me on the back, give me a worldly smile and say, "I know Pop, I already know all about it." I guess I didn't want her to go into detail.

Joe: Did you ever run into her on campus when she was with a group of friends, or some guy, a student or professor?

Grille: I only got to see her when we'd go out to a restaurant the first Friday of each month, one of our few 'family traditions'. She called it her daddy date.

Joe: When was the last time you saw or spoke with your daughter?

Grille: I started to worry last week when I couldn't contact her. I wanted to invite her to a gallery opening. Something new we could talk about.

Joe: Was she usually hard to get a hold of?

Grille: Sometimes it was a few days before she called back but it seemed to me she always made an effort to get back to me.

Joe: Did she ever disappear before?

Grille: There were long weekends sometimes. I didn't ask where she was going and she didn't seem to want to talk about it. I figured a girl her age needs her privacy.

Joe: Do you know of any friends she might visit if she needed to get away?

Grille: We're from farm country in Ohio. I think she chose Stanford because it was far away and she didn't know anyone. She could start fresh. Reinvent herself if that's what she wanted.
Joe: Why do you think she would want to change?

Grille: I'm not sure if that was her goal or it just happened. One day she's in pigtails, then she discovers boys in her teens and it's all I can do to get her to stay on top of her education. She's a smart girl. Next thing I know she's off to college, telling me she's all grown up and I have to loosen the parental strings or I'll lose her. I guess I lost her anyway.

Joe: My gut tells me she's not lost and I don't think she's hurt. I think she may be hiding out.

Grille: From what?

Joe: That's what I'm trying to find out. It could be her personal demons, or maybe someone from the wrong crowd. I don't know but I'm going to figure it out.

Grille: I wish I had your confidence. Every day that passes makes it harder for me to sleep. Maybe I've read too many mysteries in my life but all night long my brain jumps from worst case scenario to worse-than-awful. You know what people are capable of.

Joe: And I know worrying isn't going to help. You've got to keep your head clear and your eyes and ears open. If you see or hear anything out of the usual or think of anything you may have forgot to tell me, you call me at any time day or night. I'm on it 24/7.

Minus forty-five very special minutes with one amazing therapist/woman. I wanted to reassure Dr. Grille that I'd find Alex but I had to be realistic. I believe one should always give one hundred percent, unless you're giving blood but my record wasn't that good. I was a great cyber-sleuth, always have been. If it's on the internet I can find it. If it's encoded I can break it. If it's hiding behind layers of firewalls I can bring those walls down. I'm just new at the whole private investigator thing.

I was hoping to make detective for the police force until my little altercation with my, partner over, his dalliances with my former wife. I hope they're happy, terminal, but happy.

I've only had the PI license for a year and a half. I've gotten the goods on a few unfaithful husbands and wives, found a birth father for a young woman seeking her biological roots, even caught a bank employee siphoning money to a Caymans 'retirement' account. I'm off to a good start but I'm just starting and haven't much of a track record. Still, I like to think of myself as PI/Pit-bull: when I bite down on something I don't want to let go.

<u>Chapter Nine: Love Song Central</u>

I'm fallin' fast and I know it.
I'd see her every day if she'd allow it.
I'm even writing songs for her:

Hey girl, yes, you, there in the chair
Pardon me if I do my own thinking, that's fair
And I'd like to get to know you
And I'd like to know where you've been
And I would like to show you a part of me hidden within

Perhaps it's your eyes that hold me so
Maybe it's a disguise and I may never know
Though I ought to get to know you
And find where you're going to
And I ought to show you that I am a lot like you, girl

I'm dreaming that's all.
That's something I always do
And within these walls, I can be alone with you
And yes I should get to know you
if I wouldn't be so shy
Then I could show you
if I only had the nerve to try
and I don't, and I don't know why
'cause I would love to get to know you, girl

Chapter Ten: Authority Issues?

It was one of those cold for California days, windy and overcast. We opted for tea in the kitchen. Like an afternoon chat between friends that cost one of those friends over a hundred dollars but assured complete attention not to mention discretion by the other friend.

Joe: I want to apologize for the last time…

Vana: No need for apologies here. Perhaps I was a bit harsh. I have a temper.

Joe: Would you like to talk about it?

Vana: Last session, we were talking about religion and drugs.

Joe: Some people say they're synonymous. Opiate of the people and all that.

Vana: You don't like being controlled.

Joe: Or being told what to think.

Vana: Authority issues? The first forty years of childhood are the hardest.

Joe: I like to think. It's my right to think about whatever I think matters to me at the moment. And it's all just moments.

Vana: What about the future?

Joe: Haven't seen that yet. My life's filled with 'right nows' and 'now what's?' You know, I could do this's and ain't gonna do that's.

Vana: But what do you want?

Joe: Everything. Anything. Something. What do you want?

Vana: This session isn't about me.

Joe: Just once. Fair's fair. What do you want?

Vana: I want to help…people. To talk away fears, heal the hurt, open some doors.

Joe: But you keep people out.

Vana: You're here, aren't you?

      And though the session went on a while longer
           and I'm sure other things were said
      all I remember is the way she said, "you're here,"

Like she was starting to see me
      And not just see through me
          She sits there so near
             And yet far
                And all we could be
                    Is not yet what we are
                She's all give
                  And no taking
                    And I find myself aching

When I am not staring
      Sharing her laughter
          All that I'm after is her time, for real

And sometimes I want to shout
      Completely let it all out
          Whenever she asks me,
             And she always asks me:

          "Now how does that make you feel?"

Chapter Eleven: You Have Mail

The purpose of art is washing the dust of daily life off our souls."

–Pablo Picasso

Lots of young people in this twenty-first century live a part of their life in and through cyberspace. Without my website, I'd never find much work. Word of mouth doesn't cut it in the world of sleuthing or investigations. I would have thought Alex would avail herself of digital galleries for her art, visit chat rooms with a Stanford theme, post her party antics on Face-book or perhaps have created a surreal website of her own. Nada. If Stacey Space-case hadn't let me hold on to Alex's laptop, I would have missed the only lead that turned up. But there it was: You Have Mail! Someone who signed off as 'Professor X' had emailed her that she was in danger of failing her "Art and Social Change" course. I decided I might as well try to interview the guy. I knew it was a guy because he attached a photo of his butt.

My hands practically fly over the keyboard when I'm onto a hot lead. I am no hunt and pecker. By the time you can say, "Boot up or boot kick me Jesus through the goalposts of life," I had accessed the Stanford website and cyber-connected my sweet self with the school's class offerings only to find there was no such course offering as Art and Social Change. There were Feminist Art Classes, Art History, Subliminal Art, Art for Seniors, even a seminar on Art Erotica coming up. I noted the date and time in case I had the time and could find a date. There were all kinds of artsy-fartsy classes but nothing about social change. Luckily, I made a change, back to the main page, over to the faculty directory, up and down every name and almost missed it. There in the list of Visiting Fellows was one Xavier Numinez, specialist in graffiti art from New York City by way of Puerto Rico. Xavier. Professor X. It was a leap of faith but it wasn't the first or last time I would leap into something not knowing where I'd land.

Chapter Twelve: But Is It Art?

"I understand the importance of bondage between parent and child."

–Dan Quayle

Locating Numinez wasn't as easy as I thought. He didn't teach regular classes. He gave lectures and workshops. The University had given him access to the buildings and maintenance buildings. I know that sounds redundant. He didn't hold lectures or workshops in the buildings, but rather outside the buildings. He would use the building as his canvas, usually one that wasn't in line of site with a public street. He'd been given the entire wall to demonstrate his street cred, his art of the inner city, his twisted, surreal, spray paint social commentaries. I couldn't see the relevance and I couldn't find Numinez.   He didn't keep office hours, didn't return my calls, and wasn't well known by any of the regular faculty in the Art Department. It's a good thing I bothered to look at his 'paintings' on those back lot buildings or I would have missed the door.

The door I refer to was painted in Numinez' style and belonged to a run down warehouse near where I sometimes go for shooting practice to maintain my 'right to carry' license. I hate guns, but I hate the thought of being without one when someone else is shooting at me which doesn't happen often. Some husbands when caught in the act of adultery do not conduct themselves as gentlemen and are not opposed to shooting at PI's. I just want an even playing field. I keep it safely locked in my glove compartment, bullets in the trunk.

But back to the door. It was locked. There were no windows, no other doors except for two huge ones on the side of the building with a crumbling loading dock. Those doors were locked or rusted in place. The result was the same: they weren't going to move. I could come back and do a stake out but it just might be a red herring, a dead end, a stupid move, a waste of time. That's when I noticed what must have at one time been a roof crane for bringing up materials. It looked rusted and dangerous. It looked inviting. There might be ventilation structures up there. Most warehouses would just cook inside if they don't have a way for all that rising hot air to get out. And better yet, ventilation screens are much easier to get passed than a locked door. But was this going to be worth the hassle?

An hour later I was back with two newly purchased long ropes, a thin one and a thick one. I attached a metal bar to the end of the thin rope and after several tries (this shit ain't easy), I managed to throw it over the part of the crane that extended out over the side of the building. Then I used the thin rope to pull the thick rope over. Then I hoped I could remember my rock climbing knots. The old lock and loop. I fashioned a knot that worked like a brake and a loop to hold my feet. Then I could ease my way up, a few inches at a time while being able to take rest breaks. It took forever. Luckily at this time of day, happy hour, not many people in the warehouse district were out and about. I lay panting on the still hot tar of the roof in just under ten, make it fifteen minutes. I was beginning to doubt my sanity again, but not when I finally got inside through a rusted roof vent.

The place looked like a movie set for a dungeon. Whips. Chains. Swinging harness things. Sex toys and stuff I couldn't explain, didn't know about and didn't want to know. Oh, and mood lighting. The dungeon master had installed track lighting. So much for attention to detail. Now, I'm not sheltered or ignorant. I'm aware that there's a bondage scene and some people get off on it. I'm just not too clear on the details. If Alex was mixed up in this scene, disappearing for a while starts to seem like a sensible alternative.

I didn't touch a thing. Didn't want to leave my fingerprints on anything. Who knows where the thing's been? I didn't exit via the rope technique. I took the door, went around the building and shook the rope free. I should have been trying to put two and two together but as I drove home, all I could think of was what it would be like to be with her again. Even if I was paying for it. You're always paying for it. And sometimes, for a while, sometimes a long while, it's all worth the cost

<u>Chapter Thirteen: More Than A High</u>

Vana: How have you been?

Joe: Sometimes I question my sanity, occasionally it replies. Mind if I ask you some questions?

Vana: And how is that going to help you?

Joe: It'll help me to know you better. Help me to feel comfortable. To open up.

Vana: I don't know…

Joe: Could we just try? For example, what do you do for fun?

Vana: I'll answer if you do the same.

Joe: Deal. You first.

Vana: I like going to breakfast at some sidewalk café. People watching.

Joe: I could tell you're a people person. Go on.

Vana: "I like a good aerobic workout. And yoga. Being healthy. And you?

Joe: I like having music jams with people who can really play. Making up lyrics, singing, a mug of wine over ice and stinky-sticky-stoner buds.

Vana: Typical musician type.

Joe: What I'm into is creating new music. Techno-eclectic-alternatives.

Vana: You should sing for me sometime.

Joe: Shoots. (sings) Well, you can hurt a guy and you know why, it's all there for all to see and I'd crawl on my knees through Harlem babe, if you'd just spend some time with me.

Vana: OK, OK, I get the idea.

Joe: I got a million of them.

Vana: I bet you do.

Joe: I'll try to watch my sexual innuendos, but it's hard, it's so hard. Next question. What turns you on? Artistically, I mean.

Vana: Oh, a good book. Poetry.

Joe: There's something we have in common: poetry. I'm a slam poet, that damn poet who wants to move you, improve you with his love of words and words of love. To bring it, wing it past you for your consideration and poetic edification.

Vana: Did you just make that up?

Joe: I'm asking the questions here.

Vana: Yes, doctor.

Joe: Have you ever been hurt?

Vana: I broke a collar bone doing gymnastics in high school.

Joe: Have you been hurt by love?

Vana: That's personal.

Joe: Love is personal.
Vana: Have you been hurt?

Joe: You didn't answer.

Vana: OK, yes, you could say I've been… disappointed. Things don't always work out. And you?

Joe: It sort of hurt when a girlfriend left me…. for another women, not that I am a woman I mean there was this woman she left me for…

Vana: Hurt your pride?

Joe: She could have just taken me along.

Vana: Oh, that would solve everything, I'm sure.

Joe: Let's just say I've been lucky in lust, unlucky in love. And you?

Vana: I have… loved.

Joe: And now?

Vana: Now, what?

Joe: Are you in love now?

Vana: I don't see how this is helping you.

Joe: Humor me.

Vana: First answer me this. What do you want from these sessions?

Joe: I want you to tell me I'm OK. That I'm not crazy. Just as nuts as everyone else.

Vana: Alright, you're OK. There. You're cured.

Joe: Good. Now we can just talk. There's still time on the clock.

Vana: I'm speechless.

Joe: I'll just stare, then.

Vana: If you're not crazy. Why are you here?

Joe: My parents were worried about me. They think I'm depressed.

Vana: Are you?

Joe: Not now.

Vana: "Were you?"

Joe: I was. I was lonesome. I made myself lonesome, didn't want to see anyone.

Vana: Maybe you just used up all your happy juices with all the drugs.

Joe: That's always a possibility.

Vana: Joe, I want you…

Joe: Say what?

Vana: I want you to be drug free, all week, until our next session.

Joe: We could celebrate with champagne.

Vana: No, we're going to find out how you feel if you don't get high. Promise?

Joe: For you, anything.

Vana: Do it for you."

Joe: But…
Vana: Do it.

Joe: OK, OK. Reality here I come.

Who needs dope?

I can cope

My mind's my own

But why go it alone?

I asked her to sponsor me

As in, take my calls

A precaution you see

Should I fall

Hoping an open door meant

I could talk to her more

If just to brag I'm clean

Show her I mean what I say

I now know

I need more than a high to get by

I want smiles and a sigh

But I'm scared to phone

So I sit here alone with my wandering mind
And slow motion time

And obviously I'm

Not doing as well as I hope

I miss my dope

Chapter Fourteen: Any Kind Crazy

Just because I'm seeing a shrink doesn't guarantee that I'm crazy, especially considering my fortunate set of circumstances: she's hot. And on the other hand, I did wonder if I'm losing it. I can't sit in my Man Cave now that I've got a taste of the chase. And then there's the case which has been driving me stir crazy and that's a bona fide kind of crazy if you ask me. Nuts, Loco, Hog Wild, I'd cop to it all at this point.

I decided a stake-out would be better than just sitting at home. If I can think at home I can think in the car. I haven't put it all together yet but things are starting to gel. Drive through Taco Bell and I was ready. Even had tunes and headphones. A stake-out's what you make it.

I was just giving myself a napkin bath when the professor drove up in a vintage Datsun 240 Z/poor man's sport car. I was careful to have my credentials in clear view and tried to be non-threatening when I spoke.

Joe: Professor Numinez? I wonder if I could ask you a few questions?

Professor X: You're not a student.

Joe: I'm a private investigator. Joe's my name and I'm looking for Alexander Grille.

Professor X: I meet a lot of students. Some just hang out in the back when I work on demonstration pieces. I don't know them all.

Joe: You'd remember Alex. Red hair, five eight with every feminine accessory. Likes to party. Am I getting close?

Professor X: I may have met her. What's this all about?

Joe: She's missing.

Professor X: Well I'm sure I don't know where she is, so if you'll excuse me, I'd like to go in now.

Joe: Mind if I come in?

Professor X: Yes I do. Now I've tried to be polite but I have things to do.

Joe: Did you 'do' her?

Professor X: I won't dignify that with an answer. This interrogation is ended. Go away.

I wanted to take it further, piss him off and see if he'd throw the first punch. I hadn't practiced 'the thumb trick' in a while and I was itching to bring this arrogant artist to his knees. Maybe break his spray can finger. But I know better. I know I'm the one who'd get arrested and couldn't give the boys in blue a good reason why the professor was the only one with broken bones. In my line of work, I didn't need to be accused of using 'enhanced interrogation techniques'. I'm no Dick Cheney. So I walked back to my car and noticed the professor waited to watch me drive away. For somebody with things to do, he didn't seem in much of a hurry.

<u>Chapter Fifteen: No Words to Say</u>

I think of her. I write about her. She's in every song. She's in my head so much I fear doing a disservice to Alex's case. I forgot to update Vana about it the last time we were together. I'd forget my head if it weren't screwed on, when I'm with her. When I'm with her I'm walking on air. I can't pretend I don't give a damn which I am usually pretty good at doing. I've never been worried about what to say before. I want to show her this song but can't cross the line. Don't want to mess things up.

How does it feel
When you have lost your way?

What can you do
When there're no words to say?

Where do you go
When there's no place to be free?
You can depend on me.

When you're alone
And the night seems so long

So far from home
And everything feels so wrong

How do you know there will be love?
You will see
You can depend upon me

When there's no wrong or right
When there's no end in sight

Longing for love's desire
Kiss me and learn the taste of fire

<u>Chapter Sixteen: You're Nuts</u>

Vana: Were you successful?

Joe: With what?

Vana: Not getting high.

Joe: It wasn't easy. If it wasn't for the drinking, I don't know how I would have got through it.

Vana: I knew it.

Joe: Psyche! Just kidding. I had to prove it to myself. I take that back. I did it for a friend.

Vana: Who?

Joe: You. You asked me. I did it. That's what friends do. You can ask me anything.

Vana: What do you want?

Joe: Can't you see? It's not like I can hide it.

Vana: I want to hear you say it.

Joe: I want you. I can't think of anything else.

Vana: It won't work. I can't see you and…help.

Joe: Then just see me. That's help enough. You're the only one I know who can really see me at all. It's all I want.

Vana: That's what we all want. To be real. To matter to somebody.

Joe: I let you in.

Vana: It's what I do.

Joe: It's more than that.

Vana: How do we know?

Joe: You feel it. You don't have to analyze it. It's just there. It's right. It's good. Better than good.

Vana: The only thing is…

Joe: Yes, the only thing, the only thing that matters: to be real to somebody.

Vana: I have an obligation…

Joe: And I have an imagination.

Vana: You just want to play.

Joe: A play date then. You pick the playground, I'll pick the flowers.

Vana: You're nuts.

Joe: That's why I'm here.

Vana: It's not working. This is our last session.

Joe: But I need you to see me.

Vana: I see you all too clearly. You're not concerned with your mental health.

Joe: That would be crazy.

Vana: You're infatuated. You've made up this dream...

Joe: Dream with me, sleep beside me.

Vana: Doctor-patient protocols prohibit it.

Joe: It would be so healing.

Vana: You keep on saying things like that. It's not fair and it won't work.

Joe: We should try.

Vana: Alright. I've made my decision and I intend to stick by it. I can't see you anymore, professionally.

Joe: Why?

Vana: Because I want to see you…everywhere.

Joe: Dinner?

Vana: Breakfast. Lunch. Tea Time. Bath time.

Joe: What if you find out I really am crazy?

Vana: I wouldn't ask you to change. It's one of the things I like about you.

Joe: Well, Doc, I'm feeling better already.

And I really did

I kid you not

Did I mention, she's hot

And I'm willing to be all that I'm not

If it brings her joy

Boy oh, boy, did I mention?

My intention is let her be the one
Let her in

I've needed to begin again for far too long

Chapter Seventeen: What's a Romeo To Do?

For our first date, a picnic on the Stanford Quad, I brought candles, wine, pillows and a small speaker powered by my I-pod. I had recorded a song for Vana. The candles kept blowing out and getting knocked over. The sandwiches I had concocted defied explanation. It's the thought that counts and Vana appreciated the effort. I played the song, we laid down side by side, not too close but far from far and counted stars.

The candles, the wine, pillows on the floor
I forget my lines when you walk through the door

Two loves tempest tossed, what's a Romeo to do?
How can I be lost, if I'm lost in love with you, girl?

If love's not love to keep, we'll search and never find
I've been fallin' deep, yeah I'm out of my mind

It's all a tragedy when you know what love can do
And then to feel so lost, lost in love with you, girl

You say you dare not speak, that words can break your heart
A part of me's not here whenever we're apart

Words are only words but words get in the way
If you but love me, girl, there are no words to say

Cast the world aside and I'll be here with you
Love is worth the cost to be lost in love with you

Did I do any wishing on that billion star buffet? Three guesses and they better all be about Vana. She was all I could think of. I didn't want to go too fast and scare her away.

If someone had told me, before the night was over, I would be licking sweat from her tender neck, I might not have been able to calm my racing heart.

Joe: You wanna hear something crazy?

Vana: I'm off duty.

Joe: I think we should work together.

Vana: I take back my diagnosis. You are definitely nuts. Bonkers. Looney tunes.

Joe: Not playing with a full deck.

Vana: Off your rocker.

Joe: Not the brightest bulb in the box.

Vana: A couple beers short of a six pack.

Joe: OK, OK, I can take a hint. I just think it would be nice spending more time together.

Vana: Wooing, not working.

Joe: It's not that hard really. I could train you to be my Google Girl.

Vana: I can't wait to tell my mom. Six years of upper graduate work, thousands in student loans and I end up a Google Girl.

Joe: Stacked hacker? A research associate! And we could do stake outs together. We could find all kinds of fun ways to pass the time.

Vana: Aren't you supposed to pay attention to what's going on outside the car?

Joe: With you there? Now you're the one talking crazy.
(She jumps him for some wrestling, tickling, giggling, nibbling, kissy
face time)

Vana: I'll do it.

Joe: Do me?

Vana: Do it. Work with you. But I want my own desk and my name
on the door.

Joe: I don't have a desk but I do have a door. I would definitely write
your name on our basement door. In glitter if you want.

Vana: All I want is you.

Joe: Back atcha. Ready to go to work?

Vana: You don't fool around.

 Joe: I'm more than willing.

Vana: I picked up on that in our sessions. But you mentioned work?

Joe: I just thought while we're here on campus, we should cruise by
Dr. Grille's office so I can show you off.

Vana: That better be 'proud-boyfriend-speak' for 'introduce you as a
fellow colleague.'

Joe: Come on, I can see his office from here.

<u>Chapter Eighteen: Oh No, Otis</u>

Dr. Grille's office in the Language Arts Center was on the front corner of the building so Vana and I could see his light was on as we approached the building. When we got to Dr. Grille's door, I was surprised to find it not only closed, but locked. I knocked briskly and said in a loud voice:

Joe: Dr. Grille! It's Joe Freedom. I've got someone with me I'd like you to meet!

(They hear the sound of a window shattering)

Vana: That's not good.

Joe: We're coming in! (Joe tries unsuccessfully to kick the door in) Ow!

Vana: Let's both try. (they both kick and the lock gives)

Joe: Dr. Grille, are you here? (Joe goes to the shattered window)

Vana: He's over here, behind the desk.

Joe: Dr. Grille, are you alright?

Vana: His head's bleeding from more than one spot. Call an ambulance.

While I phoned for help and made it damn clear that they better hurry, Vana applied pressure to the professor's wounds, soaking up the blood with my first-date-fancy shirt. She thought he might have a concussion since he seemed only semi-lucid. Vana gave me her shirt and told me to get it wet from the water fountain we passed in the hallway. I know it was no time to notice such things, but she had on a lacey bra, tinted light purple, that she filled quite nicely.

With that image burned into my libido, I ran and soaked the shirt and returned to the office. I could hear far off sirens through the open window.

Vana began wiping the blood trails from Dr. Grille's face as I stood guard watching Vana in her bra. Hey, I'm only human and had also given up a shirt. Fair's fair. I finally had to tear myself away when I heard the EMT's entering the building to make sure they found the right office. It's the one with the broken down door. Dur.

They worked quickly bandaging his wounds and making sure nothing was broken and were soon wheeling Dr. Grille to the waiting ambulance. When I made a move to ride along I was told family members only so I grabbed Vana by the arm saying, "In that case Alex, you better go. His daughter." I gave Vana a quick wink, the door closed and I headed for my car to follow them.

I found Vana waiting in the emergency room visitors' area giving a statement to a young police officer I didn't recognize. After I repeated basically the same story, the officer took our phone numbers and left. Finally, Vana and I could talk without being overheard. "How is he?" "Out like a light, they sedated him in the ambulance. They said it helps prevent him from going into shock. You should be proud of me. Before they gave him the shot I asked if he knew who hurt him. He mumbled something about not being able to see the guy's face, that he wore a leather mask that covered his whole head."

Joe: Sounds a lot like the kind of mask used in bondage or S&M, and I know someone who's into that kinky stuff.

Vana: You do?

Joe: Don't look at me like that. I was referring to a suspect.

Vana: Sorry.

Joe: If we're going to be partners…and we are, right…?

Vana: Most definitely.

Joe: Then we've got to have each other's back.

Vana: Backs. Check. And no secrets.

Joe: None. Nada. Zilch. Ain't gonna happen.

Vana: And we need to really know each other.

Joe: Every which way from Sunday.

Vana: And I expect equal pay.

Joe: You'll starve.

Vana: You too.

Joe: Now that you mention it, I am starving. We should have eaten the sandwiches.

Vana: Then <u>we'd</u> need the Emergency Room. Let's go ring your bell.

Joe: Really?

Vana: Taco Bell.

Joe: I'm there.

Vanna: You are so easy.

Joe: Try me.

Vana: Feed me first.

Joe: But the professor…

Vana: He's in good hands. Besides, they won't ease off on the sedatives until tomorrow after they see how his vital signs are doing and check for swelling in the brain.

Joe: You sound like a doctor.

Vana: We psychiatrists have to study basic medicine too, you know. I could name every bone in your body.

Joe: You know everything you say turns me on, don't you?

Vana: Food first?

Joe: Right. We're outta here.

<u>Chapter Nineteen: Getting Warmer</u>

I bet you're just dying for details on the first time Vana and I became intimate, let the sparks fly, hooked up, did the nasty, consummated the relationship. I would tell you but words are dead, dictionaries buried, and you can't google something this sweet. Society's servers would melt. Unsubstantiated stories would plague the newsrooms of the world and journalists trying to condense her love into a headline would end up jumping from windows. It was traffic-stopping-terrific and tender in succession. But I'm not one to kiss and tell.

Ok, there was some kissing, well lots of it, in many places with remarkable results. She brought the heat, laughed in the right places, made it awesome, made it love. Nothing kinky or corny, nothing we both hadn't tried before, but I'd never felt such acceptance, which motivated my determination to please and she may have begged but she didn't need to. She could have it all. Free tickets to LaLaLand.

If I died in those arms I'd already be in heaven. Poetry and tears. She wore me out. I egged her on. I tried to sleep but then she'd touch me and I wouldn't re-enter the solar system for quite some time. I'm sorry I can't be specific. Her love defies specifics. It's a high and how are you? I'm talkin' fireworks. More dreams coming true than stars to wish on. She ruined me and yet saved my sorry soul. I didn't want to stop. Healthy all-American exercise. (I may have pulled a muscle) The taste of salt on her wet neck. "I feel so violated. Do it again."

For her I would forsake God and Country and live on air and music. Sometimes she wouldn't speak, her eyes said it all. Quiet cuddling and incredible climaxes. I poured my life's wine into her eternal chalice as angels watched and blushed. I schooled her, ruled her but damn if I could fool her. She was good, she was willing, she was helpful (I can't explain). She was laughing with me, not at me.

"Flush the weed down the john, Joey 'cause this girl is better than drugs, better than your best self". She could lift you up. Make you yearn, burn and turn from all things that are not her.

I wish I could tell you but I'm tongue-tied-tired-and-tangled. I told her, "If you love me and it sure smells like love in here, you must let me sleep or I will surely die." So, she cuddled in, made me her blanket and I left heaven for dreamland, a definite step down.

I would awake early. Rekindle the fire. She is the flame that burns and turns the only world I'll ever want. My partner, my confidant. Love to die for. It could have been a dream, a fantasy, wish fulfillment but I am convinced of its reality because frankly I'm just a bit sore.

With time, the steam cleared, my temperature and heart rate returned to normal and I could think again. Vana called to check on Otis, but he was still being kept in dreamland until the swelling in his brain subsided.

Chapter Twenty: Enlightenment Awaits

After a leisurely breakfast, I thanked Vana for her 'hospitality' which almost put me in a hospital, and hobbled off to my car and our case. I planned to hit as many rehab facilities as I could before surrendering to nature's call for a nap. I visited Pleasant Meadow Rehab Ranch, Second Chances, Bayview Consciousness Center, and Positive Cosnetics. I don't think 'cosnetics' is even a real word. I showed Alex's photo to everyone who would give me the time of day. It started to feel more like naptime with each denial. No one had seen her and some said they wouldn't tell me if they did.

I could hear my pillow calling my name but there was still one facility sort of on the way back to the Man Cave (Who da man? I da man) so I decided to give it one more try. Who knows what enlightenment awaits at the Bayview Consciousness Center? Not much view of the bay. This center occupied every floor of a ten story office building. Everywhere I looked there was marble and chrome shouting 'class act' and 'big money here!' I imagined rehab facilities that cater to celebrity types would be more like five star hotels in spa mode. Bayview was all this and more. Custom wood receptionist area, ten foot high glass doors, each outfitted with security locks. I thought I'd try the direct approach so I walked confidently, still hobbled actually, up to the receptionist's polished desk.

Joe: I'm here to visit Alexandra Grille.

Receptionist: And you are?

Joe: Here to see her.

Receptionist: May I see some identification?

Joe: Driver's? Book of the month club card?

Receptionist: A moot point really but I'd like to know who you are.

Joe: What do you mean by 'moot point?'

Receptionist: We don't permit visitors. It has proven to be un-therapeutic for our patients.

Joe: I'm concerned for her safety. Her father was badly beaten yesterday and I'm worried that someone might try to harm her.

Receptionist: And I repeat my query, may I see whatever you have in your pockets that passes for identification, or should I call for security and bring this lovely conversation to a grinding halt?

Joe: Can you just get a note to her for me?

Receptionist: I don't know who our patients are and neither should anyone else. That's what makes private facilities like ours so…private.

Joe: Surely we could work something out.

Receptionist: I'd be taking advantage.

Joe: Wouldn't be the first time.

Receptionist: It's not going to happen. If you'd like to leave your card, I could give you a call if things change.

Joe: I'll check back.

You can't seduce the satiated. Note to self, print up some business cards. As I exited, down a hallway, going away from me through a doorway, I was sure I saw a flash of red hair. It all happened too fast and far away, but at this point, any clue is worth pursuing. I'd stake out the place, maybe have myself committed, dimwitted and/or admitted. But first I wanted another run-in with Professor X. Honestly, a nap first, most likely some food, pizza preferred, then I'd start my manhunt. Little did I know that Vana had been on a manhunt of her own.

Chapter Twenty-One: A Breech of the Man Cave

When I got home, mom cornered me before I could open the basement door.

Mom: I'm very surprised, I must say.

Joe: I'm surprised myself. What are we talking about?

Mom: You could have said something. But a mother knows.

Joe: No denying that. 'Tis I who have no clue. What are we discussing?

Mom: Just because you've got a piece of paper that says you can be a private eye doesn't make you CIA. Keeping secrets is no way to treat the woman who gave you life.

Joe: As you've reminded me on several occasions. I promise to be an open book from here on in if you'd just tell me what you and I are talking about.

Mom: I figured it out. You can't hide things from a woman with my experience.

Joe: You should be a detective, not me.

Mom: I'm not always right, but I'm never wrong.

Joe: So you've told me, many times.

Mom: And it didn't take me long, even though she was only here a few minutes.

Joe: She? Who she?

Mom: She's sure a looker.

Joe: Vana? About so tall, nice…everything.

Mom: She said she just wanted to drop off a book you wanted. Said you told her she should leave it on your desk. Did you buy a desk?

Joe: Did you let her downstairs?

Mom: Let her? That woman is a force of nature, all smiles and pleasantries. I couldn't stop her and why should I? It's my basement too.

Joe: You never go down there, just kick at the door until I answer.

Mom: It saves steps. Now when were you going to tell me you're in love?

Joe: I'm in love?

Mom: Well, she sure is. You'd be a fool not to be.

Joe: Yes, boss.

Mom: I'm not bossy. I just know what you should be doing. That woman will go places.

Joe: Sounds like she already has. My inner sanctum has never been breached before.

Mom: Never been vacuumed.

Joe: I'm a mopper! Now step aside woman, I must reconnoiter.

Mom: She said next time she'll bring something special just for me. Nice girl. There's hope for you yet.

That's the last thing I heard mom say as I bounded/hobbled down the stairs to my lair, my holy of holy's, my secret clubhouse/recording studio/Man Cave. How did she find me? What did she bring me? What did she see?
 She'll drop my slob-self like a hot potato when she finds out how I've lived the past year. I've lost her. I had every intention of revealing my true self, just not all at once.

Then I saw it. Right there on the 'couch of power', a rectangular box, not too big, with plain brown paper wrapping. Rectangular and thin. It was too heavy to be a shirt, didn't rattle and was addressed to "My Partner." Cool. It must be opened. It could be a clue as to the future of our relationship. The sacred buck knife of 'Captain Camper' (an alter ego of my youthful nature boy days) was on my memorabilia shelf in the good company of my one of a kind albums (vinyl is final) and baseball hat collection. With ninja skill, I carefully slice at the wrapping tape, folded back the paper revealing a plain cardboard box. Inside the box was a tribute to my hero/philosopher and fellow mischief maker: a Calvin and Hobbes Anthology. Tucked inside the front cover was a handwritten poem/song.

I've been in love but love walked away
Such a hurtin' thing to do
I've been in all the right places with all the wrong moves
Love left me with a pocket full of blues

Darlin', haven't I told you, here's my heart, here's my hand
And forever, I want to hold you
I'm your woman if you'll be my lovin' man

I'm not askin' for a lot, just a little time
Just a moment alone with you

I've got nothin' and you've got nothin' to lose
So don't you leave me with a pocket full of blues

Why would she think I could ever hurt her? This adventure was just getting started. She must have had a bad relationship in the past. I remember her mentioning something in one of our sessions. I grabbed the anthology and melted into my favorite corner of the couch thinking this book will make great bedtime reading material but, in my condition, I wouldn't last ten pages. I knew I was heading for deep slumber/shut eye city the first time the book slipped from my fingers. Sleep felt so good. She felt so good. Life felt so good, finally.

Chapter Twenty-Two: If the Glove Fits

When I awoke it was dark, which is not easy to tell when one lives in a basement, but mine happened to have two small windows at ground level to let in light and provide some ventilation in the summer. I was eager to get back on the case before getting back on 'other things' that will not be mentioned. I still had a pizza-jones so I phoned in my order: cheese stuffed crust with sausage, mushrooms, garlic and olives. Usually I ask for extra sauce as well but that's just too messy to eat in my car. I drive a Volvo station wagon, not because I'm amused by Swedish luxury, but because it blends in. There are a lot of those older model wagons still on the road. I can even put down the seats in the back and stretch out for some brief shut eye if the situation permits.

By ten o'clock, I had pizza, two thermoses of ice water, and my tunes ready for the long haul. Without tunes, a stakeout feels like it lasts forever and my butt gets tired. If I have tunes, I tend to boogie to the music enough to improve blood flow to my derriere/ass right, the buttocks. There was no light or movement coming from Numinez' warehouse-dungeon-sex-center for the kinkily inclined. No Datsun 240Z. Not much traffic at all. By 2 am it seemed like the entire world was asleep and if I wasn't careful, I too would be sawin' a log, pushin' up Z's, chasing the Dream Weaver.

When stuck in a stake out, time drags by like an old dog with rug butt. Einstein said time slows as we approach the speed of light. He obviously didn't do many stake outs. I look at my watch wondering "What time is it?" Five minutes later than the last time I looked.

What is time really? It's something we've made up. A human construct. "Hey, buddy, have you got the time?" I'll tell you who has the time: the government. They keep it with one of those atomic clocks locked up in a museum someplace. Each day they let out just a little bit, not too much, not enough to waste, that's for certain.

But waste it we will! Many of us spend half our time wishing for things that we could have if we didn't waste half our time with wishing! You can't really keep track of time. I, myself, tend to live in the past since most of my life is there. But time keeps on a-movin'! Time marches on! Time stops for no man! Except on a stake out. My mind wanders.

To me, time seems sort of wishy washy, you know, vague, imprecise…well…sometimes.Occasionally. Usually. And I'm in no hurry. Don't like it when I have to do something right away. Immediately. At once. Just like that. The drop of a hat. Nothin' flat. No time at all.

Then there's 'sooner than you think.' That's awfully personal! Sooner than I think? How long is that? I guess it would depend on how fast I think, I think. Time on my hands my mind continues to wander and I wonder why we say 'take your time.' One of these days. Any time now. Sooner or later. Now and then. From time to time. We even have a measure of time tied to how often we procreate: a generation! And just how long is that? Well, that depends on <u>who</u> gets knocked up <u>when</u> and how often. If your grandma looks like your sister, she probably started too young.

My favorite time is "Free Time!" Now that sounds fun, doesn't it? And it should be! It's free! Doesn't cost us a penny. Ask yourself, what do you like to do in your free time? (that you can admit to… in public) And who am I to judge? Time a person enjoys wasting is not wasted time, now is it? Was this stake out just a waste of time? My butt was becoming a bloodless brick.

I decided to get out of the car and stretch my legs. I checked around the back of the warehouse. The metal frame I threw my rope over just a few days ago was still there waiting for the next installment. I had the rope in my trunk. I had no other pressing engagements. Vana had asked for a little time to recuperate from what happens when the two of us get too close. Fine. I could last a day, maybe thirty-six hours if I kept busy but I really couldn't wait to pick up where we left off. Keeping busy, that's what I'm doing, not breaking and entering.

If the place had a window I'd want to throw Numinez through it. Maybe beat him with something hard like he did to Dr. Grille. My gut told me he was the guy. Who else shows up to a beating in bondage attire?

I have no proof but I've got this rope and I can tie knots in the dark. No one's around to hear me grunt and groan as I inch up the rope, hurting in more places than I knew I had. Beat up by a girl. What is happening to me? Made it to the top. I reposition the rope so I can slide down from the roof vent like I did last time. I wish he was in there sleeping. I'd tie him up and piss down his throat (but he might like it). Maybe I should strap him into his hanging sex harness and use him for a tether ball. I touch down with only the sound of knocking over a chair that wasn't there the first time. I freeze and listen. The only one I hear is me trying to breathe quietly.

I take out my flashlight and shine a look around. Some of the professor's gear is missing. Maybe he's packing up. Moving shop. Setting up business elsewhere. 'Dungeons-Are-Us: Ask about our pain packages and beginner bondage specials'. There are now boxes everywhere, some half packed, some yet to be used. I thought to myself, I bet he's gonna run. Chicken-shit-scum-sucker. I just wish he'd show up now. I'd teach him a thing or two. The lock clicked, the door opened, and I'll be damned if Numinez didn't step inside holding a flashlight in one hand and a gun in the other.

I just had my rope. I had pulled it down after me planning to exit through the doorway now occupied by this pissed off gunman. Just a rope against a gun; now we're having fun. But I didn't take the time to wallow in self-pity. I flung that rope in his face, he fired wide and I came in kicking. I like to think of myself as a hero type but I'll kick a guy in the balls if I have to and this seemed like just such an appropriate occasion. He went to his knees, I grabbed for his gun hand trying to point it anywhere I wasn't and the son of a bitch bit me. Bit me! I embedded my elbow in his eye socket and the gun went flying. Basic officer training kicked in, contain the weapon. I leapt into the darkness following the sound of the gun sliding across the concrete floor. Numinez leapt out the door.

I finally got the gun just as Numinez got in his car and fired it up. I could have tried to shoot out his tires, but I didn't really know the neighborhood and didn't want a stray bullet hitting somebody by accident. Man, I wanted to take him on, uno on uno: Karma takes too long, I'd rather just beat the crap out of him now.

I went back in the warehouse and turned on the track lighting because I couldn't see shit with a broken flashlight… and there they were. Tucked in the top of a still open box was a pair of dark leather gloves. I couldn't find the head gear, but I was pretty sure the stains on the gloves would prove to be blood belonging to Professor Grille. This could tie Numinez to the assault on the professor and now I had enough evidence to enlist the help of my old buddies at the precinct. The gloves on the other foot now, mother hummer/kink-wad. Bite me, will ya? That creep was starting my blood to boil. He's like a 'Slinkie:" they're not good for much but they bring a smile to your face…when you push them down stairs.

<u>Chapter Twenty-Three: Pissin' on a Priest</u>

I placed the gloves in a plastic bag as soon as I got home. Mom keeps a bag full of bags in the cupboard. Speaking of Mother Freedom, as I was maintaining the chain of evidence, she sat at the dinner table munching chocolates. I tried to stay out of her line of sight but it's a small kitchen and when she saw my face she said:

Mom: I'd sure like to see the other guy.

Joe: You and me both. I won't let him run away next time.

Mom: Say no more. I want plausible deniability.

Joe: I won't trouble you with details but could I trouble you for some comfort food, a chocolate perhaps?

Mom: Goodness me, where are my manners? Of course you may have one. Just one. Go for two and I'll stab your hand with a fork.

Joe: These are the best.

Mom: She said she'd bring me something special.

Joe: She?

Mom: Are there others? You are a busy boy.

Joe: Vana was here again? When? Why?

Mom: I told you, to bring me these chocolates…and to have a little girl time, one on one.

Joe: What did you tell her? Were you talking about me behind my Man Cave?

Mom: She wanted to know more about <u>me</u>. We may have mentioned you occasionally but <u>I</u> was the center of the conversation for a change.

I told her how your father chased me until I caught him. My, did we laugh!

Joe: You didn't tell her about the baptism, did you?

Mom: Pissin' on a priest. You could go to hell for that.

Joe: Mom…

Mom: No, that didn't come up… yet. I told her, for the most part, you were a good boy…

Joe: You got that right.

Mom: I didn't mention you seeing a shrink.

Joe: Thank God.

Mom: I don't live to embarrass you, you know. It just happens.

Joe: Mom…

Mom: It's so easy.

Joe: What did you tell her?

Mom: Nothing. Nothing much.

Joe: The torture begins.

Mom: I may have mentioned one of your misadventures, when you were a kid.

Joe: How could you?
Mom: It wasn't easy. So many to choose from.

Joe: I don't want to know.

Mom: Reverse psychology won't work.

Joe: Ok, I do want to know and there are ways of making you talk.

Mom: I've already got chocolate, now if you'll excuse me, it's time for my programs. I can't believe people watch such things but it's addictive.

I sought solace in my Man Cave. Nothing seemed disturbed. No one had cleaned up, that's for sure. These four cinderblock walls surround a lair totally lacking in a woman's touch. In other words, it was perfect. I uncovered a half-eaten bag of pistachios and pretzels under carefully placed clutter and made myself one with cyberspace. My operating system was already familiar with the name Numinez (or numb-nuts as I like to call him). I checked his meager bank account. No movement there. There were only three recent credit card purchases: a meal ticket at the Dew Drop Inn Diner, then five gallons of gas at a local convenience store/gas pump, and a $389 purchase from Cheap Tickets for airline tickets. I was having a heck of a time trying to breach their firewall to see if I could find out the flight information that went with those tickets. Scuzball (another of my pet names for the Kinky Crook) was probably trying to flee the country to hide out in Puerto Rico or on to Havana, Cuba for all I cared. My cell phone started playing "Baby I'm-a-Wanchu" by Bread and my heart started rattlin' my ribcage. Vana.

Joe: Freedom Investigations. If you can pay, we'll find a way.

Vana: This is costing me enough already. Do you know what they charge for a box of good chocolate these days?

Joe: Well I know who got chocolates recently. What's with that?

Vana: Just doing what we investigators do best, gathering information.
Joe: But not on your partner, partner.

Vana: You've become a major area of interest for me. How does that make you feel?

Joe: Traumatized and energized. When can I see you?

Vana: See me…or touch me?

Joe: Torture is illegal in America, Vana. I can be there in five minutes, ten if I hurry.

Vana: But the case…

Joe: …Can wait, though we caught a break. The Master of Kink purchased an airline ticket this afternoon. Let me find out the date for departure and if it's not tonight, I'll be right over.

Vana: I'll be soaking in the tub.

Joe: Hurt me.

Vana: Can't help it. Bye.

Yes! I'm going to spend time with my favorite play pal, like a kid in a candy store, who could want more? Double yes! The plane ticket is for tomorrow morning. Look out Numinez, I am definitely not going to oversleep, if I sleep.

<u>Chapter Twenty-Four: Space To Move</u>

I could have asked Vana to come to the Man Cave but no son wants to entertain a lady with his mother walking around over his head. Besides, Vana had lots of pillows and lots more space to move and I needed to move. We started in the bath as promised then garnered support from a hallway wall before proceeding to the bed, the floor, the kitchen for strawberries, the bed again, the couch and more floor until that floor seemed like as good a place to sleep as any. We had set several alarm clocks to make sure we didn't oversleep and miss our rendezvous with the devil. El Diablo. The Kinkster. Professor Sleaze.

The sweetest words I've ever heard since childhood came whispering in my ear as morning light let itself in through the windows. "Somebody needs a bath."

<u>Chapter Twenty-Five: Consensual and Delicious</u>

We made it to the airport in plenty of time, dressed in tourist attire looking like two honeymooning lovebirds. Let's hope it pays to practice. We started our surveillance from a cafeteria table near the main concourse that everyone had to pass through to reach the gates and the TSA screening. I was famished more than my usual due to the erotic exercise provided by last night's escapades. For breakfast we shared eggs and bagels with hot tea chasers. I didn't want to take my eyes off the flow of passengers but it was hard to take my eyes off my partner. She had opted for a simple pony tail sticking out the back of a Mets baseball cap pulled low to conceal her identity. The fact that Numinez had never seen her did not come up and she looked so cute I didn't want to bust her bubble.

We were asking our waitress for more hot water when we both spotted His Sleazeness making his way through the crowd.

Vana: Suspect at ten o'clock.

Joe: It's not even eight thirty.

Vana: Over there.

Joe: I'm on it. You wait here.

Vana: The hell I will.

Joe: Wait for me.

Vana: (to Numinez) Excuse me, I'm looking for a friend.

Numinez: I'm usually available, but I've got to catch a plane.

Vana: No, I'm talking about Alexandra Grille. Where is she?

Joe: Don't think of running. I'm right behind you.

(Numinez turns to confront Joe and Vana cuffs him on the back of the head)

Vana: I asked you a question. What did you do with her?

Numinez: I didn't do anything with her…lately. I haven't seen her in days. Guess she's tired of fun and games.

Vana: Dur.

Numinez: Everything consensual and delicious.

Joe: What about professor Grille? Was that a consensual beating?

Numinez: I don't know what you're talking about.

Vana: (cuffing him upside his head again) He could have died.

Numinez: Will you call off your bitch?

Vana: (Cuffing him a third time) That one's on me!

 Numinez: (to Vana) I'm not opposed to hitting women.

Joe: (cuffing him a good one) You should be. And what about Otis? That's assault with a deadly weapon.

Numinez: Prove it!

Joe: If the glove fits we won't acquit.

Vana: Ole, O.J. We found your bloody gloves.

Joe: Can't wait to have those analyzed.

At this point the old fight or flight adrenaline was pumping through our perpetrator and he opted for both. He took a swing at me, a glancing blow and grabbed Vana, shoving her into me. We went down as gravity intended but I was careful to ease her fall with my body, knocking my head into the concrete floor, observing only momentarily all the pretty stars. Then Vana was up and running after Numinez. I had my gun with me but couldn't risk a shot in a crowded terminal. On my second attempt at rising, I finally found my balance and forged forward only to trip over a large suitcase and a family of four. Spouting apologies, I was once more hot on the trail following the blur of a bouncing pony tale and the sweetest butt I ever bit.

When I reached the exit doors I saw Vana looking in all directions, trying to ascertain just where Professor Scumbag had run off to.

Joe: Let him go.

Vana: I thought I could catch him but I guess I'm out of shape.

Joe: Your shape is fine. As for the False-Crack-Kid, he won't get far. I'm calling in some favors from some old buddies on the force. We just gotta make sure he doesn't come back and try to get on a plane until back up arrives. I think we've got enough to convince the authorities of the assault charge and that Numinez poses a flight risk.

Vana: That bastard sure can run.

Joe: Come on, I'll buy you another cup of tea.

<u>Chapter Twenty-Six: The Four F Club</u>

I don't have a whole lot of pull with the department; just a few officers willing to throw themselves on a grenade for a fallen (from grace) compatriot. We only had to wait ten minutes for back up to arrive and while we waited, sipping tea, we discussed our next move.

Joe: I think it's time for rehab.

Vana: I thought you said you were sober. That was only a week ago.

Joe: That's not what I mean about rehab. It's time for the undercover part of our investigation.

Vana: You're going undercover looking for Alex?

Joe: They've seen my face. I was thinking of someone else. Someone with nice eyes. A great personality…

Vana: I don't know. Rehab is for quitters.

Joe: If anyone knows crazy it's you and rehab is two parts crazy to one part drugs.

Vana: Well, I did write several papers on addiction in grad school. My mother has them all in labeled boxes in safe places.

Joe: Your mother sounds like my mother.

Vana: You should be so lucky.

Joe: My mom still makes cookies on a whim.

Vana: Touché.

Joe: I won't be able to control myself if you speak French.

Vana: Maybe I don't want you to.

Joe: Won't the other people in the restaurant be surprised.

Vana: What about Alex?

Joe: If she's there at Bayview, you'll find her. We're both working from the same photograph.

Vana: If she is a client and I can get to her, what do I say?

Joe: Let her know her father's in the hospital. She may want to visit him.

Vana: And what about the 'Nutso Professor'? I think Numinez is dangerous.

Joe: I think at this point, he's just trying to get away. I've got the Four F Club on it.

Vana: The Four F Club?

Joe: Former Friends From the Force.

Vana: You should have been a rapper.

Joe: Very funny.

Vana: Yes I am, but you make it so easy.

Joe: Easy. Easy.

Back up arrived: a guy I went through the Police Academy with named Barry Gates. I gave him Numinez' photo and he took over our vantage spot. Who would think a police officer with, doughnuts on his plate was actually on a stake out? We thanked him, paid for his doughnuts and coffee and headed for Vana's car, a BMW X-5 that made my Volvo look like white bread at a bagel convention. The cool thing is, and it's a guy thing, but she let me drive. This woman was looking more and more like a keeper.

Chapter Twenty-Seven: Vana Fox, Sex Addict

Vana liked the idea of going undercover though we both agreed it would be easier if she kept her real name since all her ID said Vana Fox. Besides, who more likely than a shrink to have 'issues'. I suggested an Oxycontin habit since shrinks have access to the prescription pad but she said she had something else in mind but didn't tell me any details. Bayview doesn't allow outgoing phone calls for clients for the first week of their stay so I didn't hear about her antics inside the facility. While I was busy worrying if she was OK, she was having fun playing her role. She later described her first group therapy session as follows:

Vana: Hi everyone. I mean hello. I'm not suggesting everyone's high. I'm a little nervous. My name is Vana and I'm a sex addict. Just gotta have it. That's why I'm here. Not to get some, but to try and get it all in balance before I fall off my rocker. I need to slow down. Make better decisions. Can I sit down now?

Counselor: No need to feel nervous. This is a non-threatening group of people who are going through similar struggles. There are all kinds of addictions. Learning to recognize what that means and find positive ways of dealing with our impulses is what Bayview is all about.

Rita: I would positively love to 'powder my nose' (do some coke) right now.

Counselor: Yes, Rita. Recognize. Breathe. It will pass.

Connie: I got a question for the new girl. What's your record?

Vana: I've never been arrested.

Connie: I mean your record for guys in one night?

Vana: Three but not all at once. Over the course of the evening. A date, a pick up in a club and a 'late night booty call'.

Counselor: Now Vana, we are clear that there is no fraternizing during your stay with us.

Rita: Forget Frat parties, ya can't get laid. Everyone's locked in their rooms by lights out. You can't even snuggle while ya watch TV.

Counselor: Clients tend to benefit from time alone in their rooms. It can be a time of meditation…

Sarah: Masterbation's more like it. Will that be enough for you, Vana?

Rita: Let's flip a coin. Heads I get tail and tales I get head.

Vana: I'm feeling threatened.

Counselor: Do I need to go over the ground rules again.

Edith: Respect a person's personal space, their right to be wrong, and don't make waves.

Counselor: Good summation. Now Vana, on your personal inventory you filled out before group, you mentioned a problem with bondage. When I say the word 'bondage,' how does that make you feel?

Vana: I just love the way you asked that.

Counselor: Don't avoid your feelings. They are what motivate us.

Sarah: I'm feeling a need to urinate. (points to Connie) You're an eight. (and to Vana) And you're a ten. Definite ten. Certified fox.

Vana: I thought the rule was no last names?

After everyone had introduced themselves, broken the rules and heard the rules repeated, each of the clients was given the opportunity to speak on the topic of their addiction.

Sarah related she was on very close terms with Ecstasy. A recent visit to an ER room was stimulus for admitting herself for a little R and R. Rest and rehab.

Connie liked Cocaine and found an ample supply was always available to girls who liked to give hand jobs under the table at night clubs. She was fond of saying, "I was addicted to the hokey pokey but then I turned myself around." Her father, who she referred to as Daddy Big Bucks, had encouraged the "change of scene," a euphemism for rehab in polite circles.

Rita wanted to kick a meth habit so she could get her kids back. Her life story was ghetto but her life style was Gucci. Her Daddy Big Bucks wasn't her daddy but like to be called that at the height of sexual congress.

Their counselor, Ms. Liz, had a degree in social work, a husband on disability, a teenage son on the run and a secret drinking problem. She'd be fired if anybody knew and nobody knew. Functional alcoholics are not late for work. She was the shepherd and her clients were her sheep and she was determined and uneducated enough to believe she could lead her flock to the sweet fields of sobriety. To bring the group to a centered close, she led them in deep breathing and reminded them to spend time in meditation before going to bed.

Vana approached her as she was gathering her notes to leave and asked, "Is there anyone here I can talk to who understands the lure of S&M? I feel so out to sea." "I'll see what I can do," she replied and went on her way. There was a bottle waiting in her glove compartment and a long ride home. It wasn't until the next day at dinner that Ms. Liz came through.

<u>Chapter Twenty-Eight: Walk On the Wild Side</u>

Dinner was vegan lasagna, yogurt with fruit, and fortune cookies. Vana opted to start with dessert and see what the cookie would foretell. Her fortune read: Things are not always what they seem. How ominous. How chilling. What bullshit. She was headed for the yogurt when a tall, slim young woman sat across from her. She was lovely without make up and had her flame-red hair tied back in a French braid. Before Vana could think of what to say, the woman spoke:

Alex: Ms. Liz said I should talk to you since I'm the resident freak around here.

Vana: I don't understand.

Alex: Maybe share my mantra. "I have decided to stick with love." That's a Kind quote.

Vana: So love's the answer.

Alex: Love is where the problems begin. I've been to the wild side and survived. Safe words only work if your partner isn't a fucking maniac.

Vana: What kind of kink are we talking about?

Alex: Erotic asphyxiation. Choke but don't croak. Do it right and you come like gangbusters. Do it wrong and there's a body to get rid of. I woke up with that bastard on top of me performing CPR.

Vana: Listen Alex…

Alex: Hey, I didn't say my name.

Vana: You're Alexandra Grille and I'm Vana Fox. Your father hired my partner and I to find you.
Alex: He means well but he's going to get us both hurt bad.

Vana: Too late. He's already in hospital.

Alex: Why's he in a hospital?

Vana: We believe he was attacked by Numinez trying to find out where you are.

Alex: Numi's alright in bed but not in the head. He scares me. He's why I'm here.

Vana: He's on the run. The cops are looking for him.

Alex: I want to see my father.

Vana: How soon can get out of this place?

Alex: Let's go find that out right now.

The Bayview staff was reluctant to release the two but had no legal right to hold them and when Vana threatened a rain of lawyers on their heads, the release was expedited. As soon as her phone was returned, Vana called me and I told her I'd pick them up and take them to see Otis Grille. One advantage my Volvo has over Vana's car: it can carry more than two.

I pulled up to the entrance and Vana and Alex jumped into the back seat. Normally, I'd want Vana beside me but Alex looked shook up so I figured she needed the resident shrink more than I. Vana, by way of introduction said, "This is my partner, Joe Freedom." "Sounds like a super hero," said Alex. "He's my hero alright and super doesn't even come close," added Vana. I cast a quick look over my shoulder saying, "You don't know how happy I am to see you." One thousand dollars happy. Vana must have been trying to keep her calm when she reassured Alex, "Don't worry. We're going to keep you safe."

Then BAM! Perfect timing. We were sideswiped by a speeding Datsun 240 Z driven by none other than Numb Nuts Numinez. We were shaken but not stirred.

I put the pedal to the medal and the turbo kicked in launching us into the back of his car, taking out a tail light. "I got Swedish steel, you son of a bitch and lots of it. Come on, try and hit me again." Bondage boy was more than happy to comply. He spun around in an intersection and headed straight for us: a high speed game of chicken. "Put your heads down!" I yelled as I pointed my headlights right at him. I flicked on the high beams. Might as well blind him as well as kill him. At the last minute I went right, he went left and bounced off the side of a building. I shouldn't have watched him in the rearview and paid more attention to the power pole we were fast approaching, make that contacting, steel against steel and I thought these poles were designed to break off, not break my neck which snapped forward then back, bouncing off the seat only to settle into the airbag like a clown shot out of a cannon. At the same time, Alex came flying ass-backward and managed to change the radio station with her butt. Vana was spread across the backseat trying to hold the blood in her nose and it was not cooperating.

I assume Numinez kept on going and missed his chance to finish us off. That son of a B'll be riding down 'Kiss my Ass Avenue' and screaming 'round the corner of 'No Friggin' Way.' There was not going to be any hot pursuit because we weren't going anywhere but a hospital. How convenient. That happened to be where we were headed in the first place.

<u>Chapter Twenty-Nine: If He Doesn't Find Us First</u>

Whiplashed but not whipped, we cleared the ER in record time and Vana and I led Alex up to Otis' room. Vana had her nose packed and I don't mean cocaine. She had enough gauze up her schnoz to start a small mummy. I refused a neck brace hoping instead for a pain killer lost weekend. Otis seemed to be sleeping but when Alex took his hand and spoke his name, his eyes opened and they embraced as best they could, he being attached to tubes and monitors and her being sore all over. She had two black eyes on the way.

Alex: Papa, are you alright?

Otis: What happened to you?

Alex: Car wreck.

Joe: Not my fault. I signaled before leaving the sidewalk.

Vana: Numinez side swiped us.

Joe: More than once.

Vana: He's going to need a new car.

Joe: And a new set of teeth if I get a hold of him.

Otis: Numinez is that visiting artist. You wanted me to go with you, remember Alex, just to watch him deface a building.

Vana: We think it was Numinez who attacked you. He was trying to find Alex.

Otis: I vaguely remember the guy mentioning Alex and wondering how he knew her but things got real cloudy right before the lights went out.
Joe: We're going to find him.

Otis: It doesn't matter. You found my Alex. I was worried sick about you.

Alex: It's all my fault, Poppa. I thought he was exciting and different but I didn't know different had to hurt. He threatened me. Threatened to hurt you too if I didn't do what he wanted. He kept saying suffering is good for an artist.

Joe: Been there, done that, it sucks.

Otis: I don't understand.

Joe: We believe we can link Numinez to the assault on you. We're just waiting for the forensics back on a pair of gloves. Then we can have him arrested if we can find him.

Alex: If he doesn't find us first.

Joe: That beer can didn't fall far from the trailer. I think you two need to lie low for a while.

Otis: This is as low as I get.

Vana: Your doctor said since it's a matter of your safety, you can be released to my care.

Alex: Poppa, Vana said we can stay at her folks' house until things get settled.

Otis: I'm just glad you're OK. Now let's get me out of here.

Slowly, gently, yet as fast as possible, we unplugged the professor from monitor after monitor, tube after tube, wrapped a robe around him and hustled him down the back stairs where we had a cab waiting. The cab driver gave me a quizzical look as if to say, "Are you hijacking a hospital patient? You all look like road-kill." The sound of Vana's voice reassured him. That woman could charm the fuzz off a peach, the hair off the Beatles, the balls off a bull.

<u>Chapter Thirty: Hurts So Good</u>

The first time we made love, I was sore all over the next day. The second, the same. This time, I was healing and hopeful. I suggested we get a room but Vana begged for the Man Cave.

No woman except Vana and my mom (and moms don't count) has ever entered the Man Cave. Sacred ground and dirty laundry. Microwave and hot plate. Running water and surround sound that could knock you down sound. My Comfort Cove with its cool couch/bed, lazy boy, game rocker, mini fridge and happy place mood lighting. Off limits to everyone, especially girls, an exception made for my hot girlfriend. Friend. I like the sound of that. Girlfriend. Even better.

She was kind enough to let her pained in the neck lover have the bottom. "Ow, it hurts when you move." "You don't want me to move?" "No, don't stop. Hurts so good." This was as good a time as any for gentle touch. It doesn't take much if one pays attention. A sigh. Breath on my neck. Kisses wherever it didn't hurt, never hurt.

I talk too much and will be the first to admit it, but there's so much I wanted to say to her.

Joe: I hope you don't mind if I say I love you. I feel like I wanna say it a lot.

Vana: As long as you mean it.

Joe: Absolutely.

Vana: And just what kind of love are we talking about here?

Joe: There's more than one kind?

Vana: Sure. There's the kind every little girl dreams of, puppy love, a crush or two, first love and then there's reality. There are various biblical examples. Poems and great literature.

Joe: I noticed you read the Bible. It's there on your nightstand.

Vana: So observant. You should be a detective.

Joe: You too. If you examine the good book, you'll see I left you a clue.

Vana: A clue to what?

Joe: Well, this 'love' business for one thing. I moved the bookmark.

Vana: That's right. I was reading Psalms. You moved it to Song of Solomon.

Joe: Let me read you some of the hot spots. OK, this first part would be your lines…

Vana: A lead role?

Joe: Your very own soliloquy. Here's what you say:

Have you seen the one I love?

Make haste, my beloved, and be like a gazelle or a young stag

My breasts are like towers

His left hand is under my head and his right hand embraces me

Let him kiss me

I sat down in his shade with great delight and his fruit was sweet to
my taste

You are handsome, my beloved

Your body is carved ivory

My heart moves when you speak

Let me see your face, let me hear your voice

The time of singing has come

Your banner over me is love

My beloved is mine and I am his

Vana: She seems easily won over.

Joe: Just wait, here's what he has to say about her, or I about you as
it were:

I will remember your love more than wine
        Many waters cannot quench love nor can the floods drown it.
                Its flames are flames of fire

If I should find you outside, I would kiss you,
        There I would give you my love
                How pleasant you are, with your delights.

Behold, you are fair, my love
        Let now your breasts be like clusters of the vine,
                the fragrance of your breath like apples,
                        and the roof of your mouth like the best wine
You have ravished my heart with one look of your eyes

This is my beloved, and this is my friend

Vana: There are quite a few descriptions of boobies.

Joe: Must be somewhat important, biblically speaking.

Vana: My beloved.

Joe: You make that sound so sexy.

Vana: You're easy.

Joe: Don't hold it against me. No, do.

And she pressed her chest into my face and I'm thinking this is wonderful and realizing I can't breathe but what the hell, let me die here so close to heaven and then her mouth finds mine and we mind meld melt into one creature with just one desire. Me. You. Bed. Now. Two sticks that rub together to make fire. If you are not beloved then I'm a liar. And she keeps staring into my eyes, the ultimate aphrodisiac, what a turn on. Game on.

She holds me, enfolds me in comfort and kisses. Giggles and squeezes. Licks and laughter. We two must be one. So much fun. "I have no desire, to wear clothes, around you." There are not enough words to describe her and what she can do, actually does, all because she aims to please and there goes that squeeze again and we roll. I am king of the hill but she just won't stay still and we roll onto the floor, covers and all. Love is all I have to give her. She licks the sweat off my shoulder. Love is all I have. She bites my belly. Love is all. She rests her head on my thigh. Love is her. Only her.

Hair pullin', butt grabbin' good times

Lip-biting and loud

"Undress me with your teeth."

Tempting, teasing and tickle points

The taste of those curves

Those hot spots

Let's watch porn on my flat screen mirror.

Calling all goose bumps

Naughty in the nicest ways

I could just eat you all gone as I chart the topography of your anatomy

Lip smackin' good

Tasty

Tousled and triumphant

I cry out

Her laughter filling my heart

Can I get a yes? "Yes!"

<u>Chapter Thirty-One: Rat Bait</u>

There's still the matter of Numinez. He now owed me a car, and owed Vana, Alex and Otis an apology. But how to find him? Would he come for us again?   Was I putting Vana in danger unnecessarily? His car turned up abandoned on the side of the highway. The engine block froze up when all the oil leaked from a tear in the oil pan.

He hadn't been seen on campus. He missed scheduled lectues and demonstrations. Otis had a talk with the school's dean, and though we had no hard evidence, the fact that Numinez wasn't fulfilling his commitments was enough for the administration to hold his paychecks.

Numb Nutz must know where to find me by now. He knows my first name. I mentioned that when I met him. He could have done a computer search for any private investigator with the first name of Joe. He wouldn't see my face. My avatar and myself don't look a lot alike other than both of us being well muscled and ruggedly handsome. For all I know, Professor X could have figured out where I live and put a tracker on my Volvo (God rest her soul) and that could be how he tracked us for his little game of bumper cars. I could check the wreck for any strange device attached to the undercarriage but I doubted that would bring me any closer to finding him and seeing my sweet wagon in such a state would be too traumatic.

Since Vana and I were now partners on this case, I had an honest excuse for being with her (as if lust wasn't enough). We would put our heads together and catch Professor X before the cops could. It would be fun.

Vana: Numinez is a rat and what does a rat want?

Joe: Cheese and a nice hidey hole to eat it in.

Vana: And what does our nutty professor want?

Joe: Alexandra Grille, all tied up in ribbons and bows and leather and chains and…

Vana: Then I say we set a rat trap with Alex as bait.

Joe: Do they make rat traps that big?

Vana: Come on Joe, think outside the box. Alex loves her art, right? So I think it's time she gets her own show. We hire a gallery, post some notices around the university, and see if our scuzball in rat residence comes looking for his yummy cheese.

Joe: We can't afford a gallery show. That's big bucks.

Vana: A limited engagement. Besides, one of my friends from undergrad days owns a nice little show place not far from here.

Joe: See if you can use it for the weekend. I'll talk to Alex, have her get her art together, and fill her in on our plan.

Vana: What plan?

Joe: The plan we're going to figure out…together. After a nap.

Vana: Together.

Joe: I like how you think.

Vana: This will be child's play. Every woman knows how to catch a man.

Joe: But it doesn't always involve hand cuffs.

Vana: This time it will.

No details this time.

OK, just a hint: massage oil and Pink Floyd played real loud.

By now she knew what I liked.

And yet she was full of surprises.

She bit me.

I didn't complain. Loved through the pain.

That chunk of shoulder should grow back.

What fun

But

Will I ever again get anything done?

<u>Chapter Thirty-Two: One Woman Show</u>

The Gallery was downright classy. Vana looked smokin' hot in an artsy-fartsy frock that left little to the imagination. Yum, but Alex was the scene stealer this evening in a low cut deep red dress with a slit up the side. Her hair was strewn with streaks of colors and glitter and feathers. A work of art that wiggled when she walked. With both Vana and Alex there, why would one waste time looking at the art on the walls? Here was perfection. Our trap was set and that was some beautiful bait. An hour after opening, in walks Xavier Numinez, like he owns the place. I wasn't worried about him recognizing me. I was in disguise with a fake goatee, sunglasses and gangster hat. It didn't take him long to find Alex.

Numinez: Congratulations.

Alex: You always said I should have my own show.

Numinez: But I'm hurt that you didn't send me an invitation.

Alex: I thought you liked being hurt.

Numinez: Now that's my little viper. I missed you. Where have you been?

Alex: Getting my head straight. You should try it sometime.

Numinez: I enjoy the chaos.

Alex: Different strokes.

Numinez: We're not so different. We like some of the same things.

Alex: You liked it. I just thought of it as something fun and new…until it wasn't.

Numinez: No more fun and games?

Alex: Game over, rover.

Numinez: You don't want to cross me, Alex.

Alex: I know what you're capable of. Beating up old men.

Numinez: He was keeping you from me.

Alex: I'm not your plaything anymore.

Numinez: What makes you think I'd ever let you go?

Alex: Let's just hope they never let you go.

Joe: You're under arrest Numinez for assault with a deadly weapon.

Numinez: I don't understand…

Joe: I'm only responsible for what I say, not what you understand.

Numinez: You can't arrest me.

Joe: But I can handcuff you. It says so in my license, somewhere.

Numinez: Ow, that's too tight.

Joe: You totaled my car, stupid.

Numinez: You can't prove that.

Alex: I saw your face.

Vana: I got your license number, stupid.

Joe: And we apologize if we hurt your feelings when calling you stupid. We thought you already knew.

Numinez: I want to speak with my lawyer.

Joe: When the cops are through with you. Now walk peacefully because if I lift up on these cuffs…

Numinez: Ow! Alright!

<u>Chapter Thirty-Three: Do Those Two Ever Sleep?</u>

We celebrated our first completed case together with champagne in bed. My motto: leave no delightful spot un-kissed. (note: this can lead to wet lips, dry lips and chapped lips) Later, in the afterglow, call it cuddle time, after instructing me in the ways of love she continues to instruct me in the ways of love, she says:

Vana: I will now read you to sleep with the New Testament.

Joe: Amen.

Vana: First Corinthians, verse thirteen.

Joe: Sweet Lord, lead on, read on.

Vana: If I could speak with the tongues of men and of angels,
            but have not love, I would only be making noise.

And though I have the gift of prophecy,
        and understand all mysteries and all knowledge,
            and though I have all faith, so that I could remove
                mountains,
                    but have not love, I am nothing.

And though I bestow all my goods to feed the poor,

        …but have not love, what does that say of me?

Love suffers long and is kind.

        Love does not envy.
            Is not haughty.
                Does not behave rudely, does not seek its own,
                    is not provoked, thinks no evil,
                        does not rejoice in iniquity,
                            but rejoices in the truth.

Love bears all things,
      Believes all things,
            Hopes all things,
                  Endures all things.

Love never fails.

     And now abide faith, hope, love, these three;

        but the greatest of these
                  is love.

     And I drift off, sleeping on a wet spot, thinking she is so hot.
This girl is the one.

Chapter Thirty-Four: Freedom and Fox

A new agency is born, a love kindled and I'm leaving my Man Cave behind. We're rent-to-owning a small office space with an upstairs apartment big enough for a small kitchen and a big bed. I'm sure other furniture will come as needed. I will handle the cyber-side of the business while Vana brings in cases just by sitting near the window. I feel good about this. If this business doesn't work out, we could always find another. It doesn't matter as long as we have each other. Love sure smooths out the bumps in life's road. What can go wrong when she loves me?

Professor X was brought to trial on charges of assault with a deadly weapon and terroristic threatening and will be spending several years in jail, being somebody else's bitch for a switch, painting his cell walls with his own blood and learning to be more of a criminal/scumbag.

Professor Grille is back to teaching great literature. I stop by and visit with him when I'm near campus and we engage in heated discussions on the great American Novel. He sides with *"Huckleberry Finn"* while I'm pushing Vonnegut's *"Cat's Cradle."* We both score points for greatness and neither admits defeat.

Alex is taking a semester off to work on her sobriety and her art, inspired by the fact that she sold six pieces during our little gallery night rat trap adventure. Next, she charmed the dean into a low rent/no rent deal on some work space in the maintenance yard. She had fun defacing Numinez's murals. Vana and I were invited to help pick pieces for her second gallery showing. I picked a mobile made from a smashed saxophone called "Blues No More" while Vana favored several ceramic pieces, some sculptural, some functional. Over tea she presented us with an abstract to hang in our office. It had vibrant colors and you could see all kinds of things in it. I was dumb enough to ask, "What is it?" And she replied, "It's you, a portrait of you two, the dynamic detective duo."

Space-Case-Stace will be graduating after three years in a two-year masters program. She plans to marry money and dedicate her spare time (not spa time) to any charity that catches her fancy should she ever decide to care about anyone other than her saccharin sweet self. She's medicating, meditating, and contemplating a boob job. She still thinks Alex is missing and no one bothers to correct her.

My mom doesn't deserve a mention but I know if I leave her out I'll never hear the end of it. She and Vana are thick as thieves and I imagine them plotting against me at every opportunity. She's threatening to let Dad have my Man Cave since, due to hearing loss, he listens to the TV at full blast and it's driving her nuts. She keeps asking me when I'm getting married and why am I so crazy if I have my own personal therapist? (Yes, she found that out, too.)

As for my recovery, I can honestly say I'm not depressed. Hasn't even crossed my mind. I'm the happiest I've been ever. Love has greased the wheels and I'm ready to roll. Ready to rock and roll. The only assignment I have at the moment is learning to love a lady as best I can. I am set free. I am finding my voice.

<u>Poems that almost made it into the book:</u>

It Takes All Kinds

Long live liberty!
Yes, liberty through diversity.

We the people
The American masses
The hippies and rich dudes
Pacifists, Polynesians and Portagees

Rednecks and nudists
Indians and engineers
Tweakers and toddlers

Together, we determine what it means to be
        The land of the free

Us athletes and welfare mothers
Old folks and astronauts

Farmers and free thinkers
Cub scouts and drop outs
Prisoners and pioneers

We each make up America the beautiful
    And each, in his and her own way
        Define and defend Freedom for all.

And it takes all kinds
All kinds of people
Each unlike any other
Unique so to speak

Expectant mothers
And Black Power brothers

Entertainers and explainers
Teachers and preachers
Street walkers and smooth talkers

Sculptors and dancers
Moon light romancers
Losers and boozers and crack cocaine users
Society bitches with hand me down riches

(Yes, we'll always have Paris)

The deaf, the dumb, the blind: All kinds!

Thugs and muggers
Babes in hip huggers
Bar flies and wise guys
Hipsters and tripsters

Abusive men who are all push and shove
Women who won't leave them and call that love

Politicians, morticians
Mormons on missions
Street musicians to please us
Lawyers to squeeze us

Bosses who get rich off other men's sweat
Movie stars to mollify us and help us forget

Police with big sticks
Poets with word tricks
Let's hear it for converts and convicts

Here's to the kids who go to sleep hungry
The prom queens growing cellulite
The priests with nasty secrets
All those sorry souls who live in quiet desperation
The homeless and hopeless

The shouters and doubters

Rappers with bling
Killers and kings
It astounds the imagination
How many different minds
and kinds of people it takes to make a world, this world

So, let's give thanks to the men and women
who lay down their lives in war after war
no matter what those wars are for.

Give thanks to all those nine-to-fivers
The late arrivers
The holocaust survivors
Who keep plugging away
Who are willing to pay
For our multiple sins or our marvelous deeds

God bless every soul searching soul in need
Every man, woman, boy and girl
Who make this such an interesting world.

Poem About Love

I'm a poem about love.
Well, I'm not, but this is:
Will this be followed by a quiz?
A poem about love
      and love's crazy phases
            and phrases
            and prolonged gazes.
What I mean to say is,
What I'm trying to convey is,
The big thought for today is:
      Love is more than a dream

More than part of the rhyme scheme,

but why should I philosophize
in a poem you won't bother to memorize
be we lovers or friends.

The point of this poem is,

unlike this poem,

love never ends.

About the author

Explore the literary world of Rod Martin, a multi-talented author, poet, songwriter, and playwright who lives in the lush rainforest of Kahalu'u, Hawaii. With a rich background of thirty years as an educator in Hawaii Public Schools, Rod has recently retired and dedicated his pen to creating a diverse collection of books aimed at inspiring teachers and captivating readers.

His latest book, Painted Poetry is all about combining the words of a poem with an Artwork that it inspired. For educators seeking to infuse creativity into their classrooms, Drama Games and Acting Exercises is a comprehensive guide for integrating improvisational theatre into their programs. Future Poets opens up new horizons in the world of poetry, offering over a hundred ideas for writing new and innovative poetic styles.

Rod's first collection of poetry, "Faith, Love and Hope," was recently launched on Amazon and Barnes and Noble and was soon followed by "Rod Martin's Poetic Madness" and "Poetic Reflections." Embark on a literary journey with Martin's diverse and captivating works that span across genres, leaving a smile in the hearts and minds of readers.

www.ingramcontent.com/pod-product-compliance
Lightning Source LLC
Chambersburg PA
CBHW061353310726
48974CB00001B/317